Florida's Ghostly Legends and Haunted Folklore

Volume Two

North Florida and St. Augustine

Greg Jenkins

Pineapple Press, Inc.
Sarasota, Florida

Inquiries should be addressed to:

Pineapple Press, Inc.
P.O. Box 3889
Sarasota, Florida 34230
www.pineapplepress.com

Library of Congress Cataloging-in-Publication Data
Jenkins, Greg, 1964-
    Florida's ghostly legends and haunted folklore / by Greg Jenkins.
        p. cm.
    Includes bibliographical references.
    ISBN 978-1-56164-328-8 (v. 2 :   pbk.)
    1. Ghosts—Florida. 2. Haunted places—Florida.   I. Title.
BF1472.U6J47 2005
133.1'09759—dc22   2004025871

First Edition

Design by Shé Hicks
Printed in the United States of America

Contents

Appendices

Acknowledgments

This book is dedicated to all those who have the wisdom to look beyond the confines of conventional thought, for exploring the evidence with an open mind without undo judgment in order to find the truth. I wish to thank those personalities of the supernatural, the psychical researchers and paranormal investigators who have offered me a chance to explore beyond the regions of my own philosophies. For Drs. Hans Holzer, Tony Cornell, Loyd Auerbach, Barry Taft, Kerry Gaynor, and William Roll, who first sparked my interest in the paranormal, and Dr. Andrew Nichols, Florida's own expert on the paranormal, and everyone who keeps my interest alive and strong, I thank you all for the momentum you have afforded me. I also thank Kimberly Penkava for assisting me in my journey into the unknown this last year, and Jennifer Schneider for aiding me while creating this book. Thanks to the music group *Midnight Syndicate,* whose atmospheric music not only kept me awake those late nights, but also gave me the inspirational juice to keep searching for Florida's elusive ghosts. Thanks also to Pineapple Press for having the vision to explore such topics as ghosts and the unknown. And thanks to all the many people who have helped me to make this book possible: the witnesses, the faithful, those who believe in me, and those who continue to keep Florida's unique and diverse oral traditions and enchanting folklore alive.

The purpose of this book is to create a compendium of ghostly and haunted phenomena, as well as the many enchanted or creepy locations found in the great state of Florida. It is also a registry of some of Florida's strangest and most haunted places: preternatural locations found in our cities, towns, national parks, cemeteries, and even in our own backyards. In the interest of those who wish their anonymity secure, some information, such as names and private addresses, are omitted for the sake of privacy.

During my investigations, which have taken me from one end of Florida to the other, visiting every place from lonely cemeteries, old abandoned psychiatric hospitals, and even deserted stretches of road that seemed to be endless, I found myself in awe of Florida's uniqueness. After interviewing more than eighty people in the process, I have been fortunate to learn far more about Florida's legends and folklore than I could ever have hoped for.

Of the people I interviewed, many were more than cooperative, eagerly wanting to share their stories, delighted to be recognized in some small way. Others, however, were more reluctant to share their personal accounts, wanting to remain completely anonymous. The reluctance of the latter group of people is generally due to their livelihoods, positions in their towns or cities, or understandable insistence on not revealing their personal addresses. Other stories and locations, however, are revealed for the reader as an invitation to do his or her own ghostly investigations and to consider this book a personal guide to some of Florida's most haunted localities, where ghosts abound in very unexpected places.

Preface

The subjects of ghosts and haunted locations, life after death, and the shadows we sometimes see in the corners of our eyes were discussed to some length in *Florida's Ghostly Legends and Haunted Folklore, Volume 1, Central and South*. I offer here a few more dark and creepy legends from the Sunshine State. Indeed, while researching these many ghostly legends and oral traditions, I have come to believe that there is an almost unending supply of such folk tales.

In Volume 1, I explored the many dark aspects of Florida's particularly impressive haunting folklore—tales that inspired more dread than mere folly. Some stories have been passed down from family to family and focus on a spirit who is more than likely a member of that family; other tales stand out to the general population because they involve remnants of a torturous time or an existence of pain. Either way, these spirits and specters appear to be far more than heated imaginations or simple nonsense. In most of my exploration, collection, and analysis of these ghostly tales, I have found there to be a singular sincerity among the storytellers that should not go unnoticed.

As I interviewed literally hundreds of people in the last two years, people from all walks of life—homeowners and morticians, historians and policeman—I was afforded the chance to see a different side of these time-honored legends. Undeniably, I found myself being fueled by the intense aspects of Florida's history, both the good and the bad. And, as a result, I was led to even more of the dark regions and creepy avenues in this great state.

In Volume 1, I had the opportunity to visit some of Florida's most exotic and beautiful locations. When exploring the sheer grandeur of the Biltmore Hotel in Coral Gables, I was amazed by the colorful history of this charming hotel, as well as the turbulent past that many people have forgotten, or never knew at all. The exploits of the 1920s gangster "Fatty" Walsh and the Biltmore are legendary, and his spirit today is no less a notable figure, and just as much the ladies man as he was so many years ago.

When dining at Cap's Place Island Restaurant in Lighthouse Point, I found more than just a wonderful meal. The distinct presence that so many feel there, as well as the scent of old cigar smoke wafting through the air, certainly had me looking over my shoulder, waiting for old Theodore "Cap" Knight to walk out from the bushes. And, as I toured the Boca Raton Resort and Club only a few miles up Federal Highway, I couldn't help anticipating the jovial Addison Mizner strolling the lush and ornate foyers of this gorgeous hotel, or the trusted Esmeralda tending to her host, leaving the scent of roses wherever she went. South Florida truly is a golden coast, and a good bit haunted, as well.

When investigating central Florida, from Tampa Bay and St. Pete to Orlando and Cocoa Beach, I found myself in awe of the simple rewards of nature's beauty, and of the laid-back nature of many Floridians. But there is more than just beauty and a relaxing attitude to be found there. Central Florida's history will certainly speak for itself, and yet, there appears to remain an unseen reality in our state's history, which sometimes shows itself to the unsuspecting.

As I drove over the Sunshine Skyway Bridge early one morning, I had hoped to see the hitchhiking ghost of a young girl who always searches for a ride to the other side. I was gripping my steering wheel tightly as I remembered the horrible tragedy that took place there in 1980 and the many lives that were lost that early, foggy morning. When I walked through the huge marble mausoleum of the incredible Myrtle Hill Cemetery near Ybor City, knowing that I was the only one there those late evenings, I did indeed hear the low whispers and out-of-place voices coming from the cold, dark recesses of this giant tomb . . . an experience that had me walking out of that scary place in a hurry, with the hair on my neck standing on end.

To be sure, as I explored the many haunted locations that Florida offers, I knew I had to keep exploring further. As I did so, I traveled up each coast, surveying and collecting stories, in search of other time-honored oral traditions that would otherwise remain hidden. Traveling to tiny hamlets like Micanopy, where you'll find the charming Herlong Mansion and the mothering spirit of Inez Herlong-Miller, and to the opulent St. Augustine, the crown jewel of Florida's past and present where there are likely to be more ghosts here than anywhere else in the United States—I was fortunate to have seen Florida at its best.

Volume 2 will take you even further into the Sunshine State's haunted realm, and once again, what you read might just have you looking a little closer at what was once taken for granted. Although Florida still offers the beautiful beaches and lakes, the gorgeous hotels and landmarks, and of course excellent universities and cultural institutions, there is still something else here . . . something downright supernatural.

Perhaps all the things we see and speculate as the spirits of the dead may in fact be nothing more than our imaginations. Perhaps the whispers and disembodied voices are nothing more than the fear of the unknown, or an innate belief in the otherworldly. Perhaps this is true, but there is indeed evidence for a world that co-exists with our waking state that for some goes unnoticed, and yet for others is seen, heard, and experienced as absolute reality. For some, ghosts are as real as you and I, able to inhabit our realm as easily as we do. And although there are those that will argue that ghosts are something explainable in scientific terms, there are others who choose to look beyond the fringes of the rational and what we consider to be reality, actively looking for the unexplainable.

With this said, I invite you once again to prepare to go beyond Florida's bright, sunny days and vacation spots and step into the lesser-known, darker areas of our most haunted Florida.

Introduction

More Legends and Beliefs

Is all that we see or seem but a dream within a dream?
—*Edgar Allen Poe*

The concept of fear was a powerful reality for Edgar Allen Poe. Poe's life was filled with the tormented ghosts of his past and the unfortunate specters of his present, and his entire world was truly haunted. Poe was a man with an almost uncanny understanding of the afterlife—not only did he believe in supernatural legends, but he surrounded himself in a world of graveyards and old abandoned mansions that sat on barren mountains, of overgrown valleys and dales. Indeed, his was a mind of both the mysterious and the preternatural.

Perhaps for Poe, the ominous, creepy subjects of his stories and poems were to some degree true—strange encounters in his life left their impressions for his creative writings to elaborate. In this tradition, our imaginations may create strange and frightening things such as ghosts and hauntings, events which may have earthly explanations. There are some incidents that cannot be explained no matter what, incidents that will eventually become tales to be told by the fireplace, then local history, then legends passed down through generations. Time changes the story piece by piece until only small fragments of the original tale remain. After undergoing the sometimes subtle, sometimes great degrees of alteration, what is left is oftentimes far scarier than the original incident the legend was based on. So form the ghostly tales we all know and love.

Although people today are certainly more skeptical toward supernatural occurrences, and belief systems have been altered over the years, the ghost story still has the power to intrigue. Although many of us simply disregard the idea of ghosts and hauntings as nothing more than the fearful leftovers from our primitive past, refusing to entertain such stories as anything more than fiction to be told around campfires or on stormy nights, there are still those who believe.

Legends of haunted houses and restless spirits are sadly becoming a forgotten aspect of our culture today. Perhaps our high-tech computers and cell phones are taking much of our time away from us, or perhaps reality TV is replacing a good book. Yet, for some, the supernatural legend still has the power to invigorate the imagination and propel to further research, exploring the sources of such legends. Some are inspired to open their minds to many other philosophies and aspects of their reality regardless of their high-tech world. Indeed, some may find the hidden truth to these and other legends through their exploration. For most, however, without tangible evidence for the existence of ghosts, such flights of fancy shall always remain in the ethereal realm of the unknown and within the obscure, untapped regions of the imagination.

Beyond all the paranormal elements of our legends, however, whether they are ghosts or mystical creatures, the one thing that all of us question, regardless of race, religion, or status in life, is the fate of our consciousness after the death of our physical body. Do we truly cease to be, or do we go on to some heavenly place of existence? Anthropologists tell us that humans have always asked this question. Do we go to a higher plane of reality, or do we simply rot in the ground? Without a doubt, this is an age-old question that either falls within the realm of faith, or is simply ignored due to fear of the unknown.

Those who refuse to believe that we simply die and return to earth will ask the aforementioned questions for the rest of their lives. Those who have no doubt that life continues in another reality will undoubtedly continue searching for an answer. Edgar Allen Poe questioned these ideas throughout his life, always preparing for death, and fearing it with great intensity. He felt it necessary to delve into the morbid and the macabre, making it into his very reality, actually concentrating on his fears. Publicly, Poe believed that the very concepts of ghosts, spirits, or apparitions were most often, if not always, nothing more than mental aberrations, embellishing the realms of fantasy. Yet, in his private thoughts, he would often wake up in cold sweats, claiming to have seen and heard the dreadful remains of the angry, vengeful dead. His fears were so great in fact, that he outfitted his future coffin with a special bell and chain just in case he was buried alive, which was his greatest fear.

Although Poe might exemplify an extreme of this natural human fear of the unknown, and death particularly, many people today seem to occupy the other extreme, finding a place to put their fears, even denying the concept of life after death altogether. For some, however, the belief is all too powerful and real. Indeed, many scholars and religious leaders alike believe that the human spirit may separate itself from its mortal host and exist separately for anywhere from a few moments to many centuries. Each spirit has its own purpose and time among the living, and the manifestations, too, vary according to the individual purpose of each spirit.

Spooks and specters appear to have many different guises, and certainly there are many forms that have been reported over the years. One of the types is the crisis apparition, a spirit said to show itself to a family member as a warning of danger, or to give assurance that the person in question did indeed die and is either at peace or has unfinished earthly business. Other forms of ghosts or entities may seem to reiterate their concerns by steadily repeating a particular action. These spirits are said to be the residue or "spiritual recording" of a person rather than an actual sentient entity. An example of this phenomenon is the cliché of the ghostly soldier who walks the ramparts of an ancient fort, seemingly always on duty, conducting the same motions and behaviors every time he is spied. In the first volume, I spoke of such a phantom who walks the remains of an ancient fort in New Smyrna Beach. This long-dead Spanish soldier might be seen walking back and forth on stormy nights, as if keeping lookout for enemy ships at sea, only to disappear when approached by the living. Many paranormal researchers and psychics believe that this soldier is simply a recording of something that took place long ago, not necessarily a sentient being.

A haunting of a home, apartment building, or supermarket, or any place for that matter, is of course the most represented supernatural event in television and film. A classic haunting might have all the customary attributes, such as eerie cold spots, a creaking floor board, a door that will open or close by itself, perhaps the sounds of footfalls in an empty house, and even strange or revolting smells where there should be none. All these oddities may constitute a haunted location.

As stated before, haunted locations can certainly be homes or apartment complexes, but they might also be crowded department stores, hospitals, theatres, and of course cemeteries and battlefields. All such places can have preternatural residues or vibrations of tragic events from the past. Some places are even believed to house a portal for ethereal entities to come and go as they please. Additionally, some believe that if you build a home over a particular location, such as a burial ground, battlefield, or other place where horrific events have taken place, you might just be inviting the supernatural entities into that home. In fact, many practitioners of the paranormal believe the whole world is haunted, complete with complex arrays of supernatural highways and byways. In any case, this book is for those who believe in spirits and haunted locations, and even for those interested skeptics.

As Florida is certainly full of such supernatural highways, it seems likely that ghosts and similar entities co-exist right along with us. And, because there are so many examples of eloquent legends and oral traditions that have been passed down over the years, perhaps the stories of Edgar Allan Poe were indeed based on fact and personal experience.

With that said, prepare yourself to enter a darker, spookier Sunshine State—what I call Haunted Florida.

1. The May-Stringer House, Brooksville
2. Silver Springs, Ocala
3. The Herlong Mansion, Micanopy
4. Hotel Blanche, Lake City
5. School Four, Jacksonville
6. Chelsea Courtyards Apartments, Jacksonville
7. Homestead Restaurant, Jacksonville
8. The Casa Marina Hotel, Jacksonville
9. Mayport Village, Mayport
10. Site of Sunland Hospital North, Tallahassee
11. The City of St. Augustine
12. Castillo de San Marcos, St. Augustine
13. The Old Spanish Hospital, St. Augustine
14. Flagler College, St. Augustine
15. Casa Monica Hotel, St. Augustine
16. St. Francis Inn, St. Augustine
17. Casa de la Paz, St. Augustine
18. Casablanca Inn, St. Augustine
19. Harry's Seafood Bar and Grille, St. Augustine
20. The Florida School for the Deaf and the Blind, St. Augustine
21. Huguenot Cemetery, St. Augustine
22. The Old Jail, St. Augustine
23. The St. Augustine Lighthouse, St. Augustine

Site Map

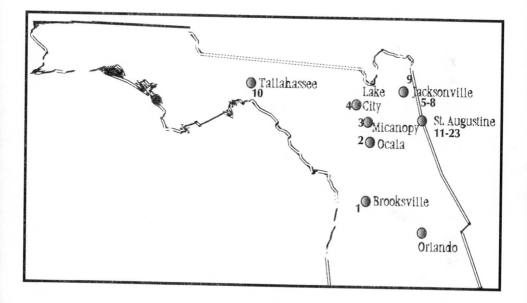

Tallahassee
10

Lake City
4

Micanopy
3

Ocala
2

Brooksville
1

9
Jacksonville
5-8

St. Augustine
11-23

Orlando

North Florida

1

The May-Stringer House

Brooksville

Don't Make Jessie May Mad!

A Little History

The May-Stringer Heritage Museum (also known as the Hernando Heritage Museum), a majestic Southern antebellum home with seven gables and gingerbread trim, is located at 601 Museum Court in Brooksville, Florida. Built in 1856, this home has four stories and twelve rooms in all, a large country kitchen and an adjoining summerhouse kitchen toward the rear of the home, all decorated in a Civil War–era motif with over 10,000 pieces of antiquity on display. The parlor room is reminiscent of the high Victorian style, complete with a foot-pump organ. A large porch surrounds most of the house and is lined with rocking chairs, giving it a true Southern look.

Because the May-Stringer House is a museum, all the rooms hold artifacts from Brooksville's past, including a few pieces of Florida's first telephone and switchboard equipment, as well as a medical examining room, complete with an examining table and cases filled with various medical antiques. The museum also has a small schoolroom and a library, which was once used for local children, as well as an attic filled with many examples of Florida's history that give the viewer a peek into what life must have been like living in Florida 160 years ago. It is truly an educational experience.

Mr. John May once lived in the house with his wife, Marena. After John died, Marena remarried Frank Saxon and the two had a daughter, Jessie May. Sadly, Marena died giving birth to Jessie May; and worse, Jessie May would die only a few years later at the age of three. After several years, Mr. Saxon moved away, and a Dr. Sheldon Stringer bought the house to serve both as his home and for his medical practice. Dr. Stringer altered the home by adding a room for his patients and even had a special exit constructed so that his patients could walk directly out of the exam room without disturbing the doctor's family.

In September 1877, the Brooksville courthouse caught fire and burned down, destroying all records concerning the May-Stringer house. The May-Stringer house and its land was donated to Hernando County, and a new courthouse was constructed next to the home. The house still stands, practically unchanged from the nineteenth century, and is listed on the National Register of Historic Places.

Today, this charming home is lovingly maintained by several of Brooksville's residents who volunteer to recreate the environment from America's early years. These volunteers guide visitors around each of the rooms and describe what life was like then. And although they'll let you walk around by yourself to get that Southern, homey feel, don't be surprised if you get the feeling that someone's watching you, as this home seems to have something more than just antiques and quaint decorations within it. The May-Stringer House, a gentle reminder of a more civilized time, seems to have a ghost residing in it—the ghost of Jessie May Saxon.

Ghostly Legends and Haunted Folklore

Every volunteer at the May-Stringer House, if not the entire town of Brooksville, knows the story of Jessie May, the daughter of Frank and Marena Saxon. The child was born in the house, and eventually died in the house when she was only about three years old. Although she never knew her mother, Jessie May was said to have missed her so terribly that she would wake up in the middle of the night and walk around the house crying out for her. Some believe that when she got sick, she willed herself to die in order to find her lost mother. Apparently, though, she never did, as her spirit is believed to wander this beautiful home even today.

When I visited this site in 2003, I already knew about the ghost of Jessie May, as the May-Stringer ghost story has appeared in several publications. There's no doubt that many people have heard the legend of Jessie May, and when I finally got the chance to see this allegedly haunted home, the feelings of something otherworldly were indeed quite strong. When I walked around the home with the volunteer guides, I took the opportunity to ask questions about the haunting and what type of experiences, if any, they may have had. The women who work there are middle-aged, refined people who are quite open with their opinions regarding the paranormal events. They are anything but wide-eyed, blithering fanatics on the subject of ghosts; they have a down-to-earth, matter-of-fact way of describing their experiences. And their opinions are unquestionably affirmative—there is definitely a ghost there.

On most occasions, the May-Stringer ghost is not dangerous, but she is without a doubt particular, especially if you move things, like her toys, from where they should be. Many of the Victorian-era toys are on display in the dining room and the surrounding parlor area. These toys, mostly wooden objects and dolls, are occasionally rearranged or displayed on another floor by a volunteer. The next day when the volunteers come in to work, there's a good chance they will find the toys scattered around the room in disarray. What they find always looks as if a child had a temper tantrum. As the home is locked securely and monitored by an alarm system, someone breaking in to make a mess like this just doesn't make sense, especially when nothing is stolen.

When visiting the second floor and looking into Jessie May's crib, you will find a porcelain doll, complete with nightgown and delicate face. This doll sits serenely on the pillow within the crib and stares out as if in contemplation. If you're tempted to pick up the doll, please do not—not so much because it is an antique, but because Jessie May will not like that. According to the volunteers here, a helper once moved the doll from the crib to the nearby bed. The next day when one of the ladies came in to the bedroom, the bed sheets had been pulled

back and articles of clothing had been thrown around the room. There was neither sign of a break-in nor any other form of vandalism in the house, which naturally made the whole event even stranger.

On another occasion, the attic appeared to be the scene of a poltergeist outbreak. Again, when volunteers arrived for work, they found the attic space completely disarranged; specifically, a toy cash register and its play-money contents had been scattered around the room. This particular toy, unlike the Victorian-age toys, was more modern, no more than twenty years old. Perhaps Jessie May was somehow offended by this modern toy with its paper dollar bills and plastic coins. While other parts of the room were also disarranged, mostly boxes and pillows tossed to the floor, the toy cash register seemed to be the primary focus of the mess. It was on its side, as if kicked over, and all its contents were littering the floor. Although these paranormal behaviors are certainly frightening, most of the sprit's rearranging has been less violent. Sometimes an object like the doll or another toy is moved as if another volunteer had just wanted a change from the usual and placed it somewhere else. Needless to say, these rearrangements can cause confusion among the museum's staff and add to the overall mystery of the mischievous May-Stringer ghost.

Not long ago, right before Mother's Day, the volunteers displayed several teacups on a small table that sits in front of the fireplace mantle. When the volunteers had returned the following morning, there was one extra teacup added to the original setup, and the day after that there was yet another cup placed there. After looking around for the origin of the teacups, a volunteer discovered that they had been moved from the china cabinet to the table. There was a scheduled tea party for some of the town's ladies in honor of Mother's Day, and some feel that Jessie May wanted to add as many teacups as she could, so that maybe, just maybe, her mother would come, too.

Recently, a volunteer arrived earlier than normal, around 7:30

A.M., long before the museum opened its doors at noon. The volunteer claimed that she heard loud noises coming from the attic. She knew that nobody else should be in the house this early and was naturally a little frightened. Everything was in place and undisturbed on the first floor, so she decided to be brave and creep up the stairs to see what was going on. As she was turning for the attic stairs at the end of the second floor, the noises seemed to be dying down, and when she got to the top, the noises had stopped altogether. When she opened the door, she found that many of the boxes were moved and some old magazines had been thrown across the room. The volunteer believes that Jessie May was upset to have been disturbed so early in the morning.

Although the spirit of Jessie May becomes upset from time to time, the most disturbing aspect to her legend is the pitiful, woeful lamenting of a lost child. On windy days, or when loud noises permeate the house, such as from a vacuum cleaner or a power drill, witnesses have heard faint but recognizable crying. Sometimes, people can hear a distinct voice calling out "Momma . . . Momma," followed by weeping, then fading to nothingness. These sad cries have been heard throughout the stately home by many people over the years—not only by the volunteers, but also by the many visitors from Brooksville and abroad. Jessie May had been looking for her mother even before she died, and many psychics and other paranormal investigators feel that the strong bond between a mother and child may follow to the afterlife. Moreover, because Jessie May had expired in a state of grief and confusion, perhaps her spirit got lost between our existence and the ethereal plane. Even though Jessie May and her mother are buried next to each other on the grounds of the May-Stringer House—in the front lawn, in fact—they have never found each other in the afterlife, which has apparently resulted in this museum's uncanny reputation for ghosts and paranormal activity, leading to the legend of the spirit of a lost little girl still searching for her mother . . . the legend of Jessie May.

Afterthoughts

The May-Stringer House is more than a museum; it is a portal to Florida's frontier past, where life was always a challenge, and where comforts were few and far between. With the ravages of the Civil War and the many diseases that spread like wildfire in those days, it stands to reason that there would be a lot of turmoil, death, and sadness within a house from that time. A story like Jessie May's is not uncommon, as Florida's antiquated cemeteries are full of families that were wiped out by such hardships.

When you visit the May-Stringer House, take the time to walk around the attic, and see if you will get the same feelings of being watched as so many have before. Walk through the downstairs parlor and gaze at the Victorian furnishings and the photographs near the beautiful fireplace. If you find a photograph of a sleeping child then you have found Jessie May. It is a serene, almost pleasant photograph, but you will quickly notice that Jessie is not just sleeping—this photograph was taken while she lay in her coffin the day of her funeral.

Parapsychologists and psychical researchers have come here to look into the ghostly goings on, and many of them claim to have found evidence of something out of the ordinary. Although the paranormal events at the May-Stringer House are usually mild, events such as teacups being found in a place where they should not be, and the bedroom and attic being ransacked from time to time by unseen culprits, point to classic poltergeist phenomena. However, most poltergeist activity is short-lived compared to this haunting, and so the remarkable events in the May-Stringer House may continue for centuries.

The fact that both Marena and Jessie May are buried in the front yard is not uncommon, as a family cemetery on private land was customary for many years until there were legal changes to bury the dead in designated places. Although there are no markers or gravestones here, there is a slight depression in the ground just beyond the sidewalk, before the front steps leading to the house; so be careful where you walk—Jessie May has been known to throw a tantrum from time to time.

2

Silver Springs

Ocala

A Watery Tomb . . . An Eternal Love

A Little History

If it's nature you're looking for in a theme park, then Silver Springs is for you. This all-natural oasis has been a sanctuary for centuries. With its pure bubbling springs—the world's largest clear artesian water source—and abundant wildlife, Silver Springs has been and remains one of Florida's unparalleled beauties, not to be missed.

The Timucuan Indians lived here in the sixteenth century and called this paradise "Ocali" until the invasion of the Spanish militia in 1539. Although Hernando DeSoto and his Spanish army were mighty and well equipped, the Timucuans were at first victorious. But eventually the simple lifestyles disappeared, and quiet rivers became the busy industrial lanes of a new era.

By the 1930s, Hollywood found Silver Springs to be of interest, too, as the scenic beauty and untamed, rugged look it offered was ideal for such films as *Tarzan, The Creature From the Black Lagoon,* and *The Yearling.* The popular 1950s television series *Sea Hunt* was also filmed here, making Silver Springs a hotspot for filming underwater scenes.

Today, Silver Springs is known primarily for its natural beauty, the wildlife in the forest and the crystal-clear waters, and of course, the famous glass-bottom boats. This land was the location of so much history, both peaceful and violent, so it stands to reason that such intense feelings would culminate in the ghostly vibrations and apparitions that many claim to see. In fact, when such feelings are as strong as those felt during war, or upon finding true love, such feelings are said to leave an indelible pattern. Many believe such feelings scratch on the very fabric of the human consciousness, which can sometimes be seen and felt long after death. This may be the case with the timeless love story of Silver Springs and its haunted "Bridal Chamber."

Ghostly Legends and Haunted Folklore

I remember hearing this story years ago when I was visiting Silver Springs during a summer break. It was while we were on one of the glass-bottom boat cruises that the tour guide told the story. We were over the exact location of the Bridal Chamber, as it is called, where the ghosts of two lovers are said to remain.

As the legend goes, there were two young people who were very much in love. And, much like a Shakespearean tale of forbidden love, these two were fated for romantic tragedy. Although there are a few different versions of this story, I will expound on the one of them that seems to be the most accurate according to local historians.

A young man, Claire Douglass, was the handsome son of Captain Douglass, a tyrannical landowner known for his brutal treatment of the local sharecroppers. Captain Douglass was also one of the wealthiest men in the area, and a member of Southern high society. Claire, in contrast, was a kind and understanding young man to everyone he met, thus creating an rift between father and son. Claire was unfettered by his father's power and held on to the simple, sentimental things, like a gold jewel-studded bracelet given to him by his estranged mother.

Bernice Mayo was a beautiful young girl with long blonde hair, a native of the Silver Springs region and known for her happy, carefree outlook on life. She had been searching for that someone special to spend her life with. Although she was a kind and gracious girl, she was from a poor family. Of course, the wealthy society in those days held itself high above the working class, the poor, and the commoners, regardless of the issue of love.

After a falling-out with the cruel Captain Douglass, young Claire spent time in Silver Springs to gather his thoughts and to calm his anger with his father. It was during this time that Claire met Bernice. They developed a wonderful friendship that naturally grew into a pure, unadulterated love, which would, evidently, last an eternity.

Claire and Bernice would go to a pleasant spot in the river called Boiling Springs, and sit in a rowboat, embracing for hours. It was there that Claire pronounced his undying love and proposed marriage. Not having an engagement ring, he gave Bernice his mother's family heirloom, the golden bracelet, as his token of love and a sign of their betrothal. Happiness seemed to be endless for the two lovers. But the cruel Captain Douglass was totally against the marriage of his son to this poor country girl.

Captain Douglass, so angered with his son's choice for marriage, had Claire shipped abroad until he could come to his senses. In those days, even with the obvious independence of young Claire, he was obligated to obey his father and leave for Europe. Proclaiming to Bernice that he would return for her, and that he would write daily, he obeyed his father's wishes and departed from the one he loved.

As Bernice waited for her love to return, she looked forward to any correspondence from Claire, yet no letter arrived, no word of any kind. Apparently, Captain Douglass intercepted the letters first, and being the tyrant that he was, would give no word at all to Bernice. Thinking Claire had forgotten her, she sank into a deep state of depression and soon fell ill—physically, mentally and spiritually. She felt she had nothing to live for.

At this point the legend seems to fluctuate. According to some of the locals of Silver Springs, Bernice rowed out to the spot where she and Claire had spent so much time embraced in their passion for each other, and, in a fit of depression, slipped overboard to her death. Others say that Bernice became seriously depressed and willed herself to death, then was lovingly placed in the waters of Boiling Springs by her nursemaid and friend, Aunt Silla. Either way, Bernice became a permanent resident of Silver Springs.

As this tragedy ends, Claire returns from abroad to wed his beloved, only to learn of her death and her place of burial. His loss was so devastating, he hurried to Boiling Springs to contemplate his woe. At that point he saw the glitter of his mother's golden bracelet eighty feet below, the same gold bracelet he had given to Bernice months earlier. Desperate, Claire dove into Boiling Springs to bring his love to the surface for a proper burial.

Unfortunately, Bernice's lifeless body was stuck on the rocks below, making it impossible to bring her up. With this frustration, and his sadness ever-growing, Claire decided to remain with his beloved in the depths, forever together as one. As legend has it, the rocks below opened up and swallowed the lovers.

Year after year this timeless love story is told and retold to visitors and locals alike. From time to time when peering down over the Bridal Chamber from a glass-bottom boat, you just might see the two lovers, still embraced in their eternal love. Some say they have seen the two walking the banks of the river hand-in-hand, both happy and carefree. Some tell of the reflection of Bernice smiling through the glass bottoms of the riverboats. The legend has lasted many a year, and although the two lovers could not be together long in life, their love surely lives on in death.

Afterthoughts

When we think of all the history that took place in this beautiful park, from the ravages of the Indian wars and the countless deaths that lay in the wake, to the yellow fever outbreak that killed hundreds, countless instances of pain and hardship come to mind. With the emotional bliss of romance leading to the tragic loss of love, it is not hard to believe that such emotions could last beyond death. Claire and Bernice created so many intense feelings in those brief months they had together—feelings that were even more powerful than war, hatred, or fear—that many believe their short romance stirred an uncanny phenomenon that will last forever.

When visiting Silver Springs and the bubbling waters of the Bridal Chamber, remember to gaze fondly on their resting place, and perhaps, just perhaps, you too might glimpse Bernice's flowing blonde hair moving back and forth with the waters below. Perhaps you will spy the lovers embrace, a testament to all who see them that love is indeed eternal.

3

The Herlong Mansion

Micanopy

Inez

The ingredients for a good ghost story are all in place here, a majestic old Southern manse with secret rooms and a tragic past, dark nights and huge oaks draped with Spanish moss that sway in the wind . . . the ghost here is said to be that of Inez Herlong-Miller. . . .
—*Herlong Mansion brochure*

A Little History

Micanopy, Florida, located between I-75 and US-441 in southeastern Alachua County, just south of downtown Gainesville, is one of the last outpost-like towns in the state of Florida. Micanopy (pronounced *Mick-can-OH-pee*) is a small, one-stoplight town where the streets are lined with ancient oaks covered with Spanish moss. Surrounded by stately homes and small storefronts, this town reflects the very nature of the word quaint, where time seems to stand still. With small antique stores and old bookshops, and the small family-owned emporiums that offer handmade ceramics, stained glass, and jewelry, the town is truly a portal to a more civilized time. The bed-and-breakfast inns and gourmet restaurants offer small-town values and hospitality

14

that will make anyone's stay enjoyable.

Micanopy is also considered one of the oldest native inland settlements in Florida. Ancient documents show that a village was discovered here in 1539 by famed Spanish explorer Hernando DeSoto. In fact, the Timucuan Indian tribe is believed to have lived in this area for thousands of years. The first European settlers arrived in 1821, bringing Western civilization to Florida, adopting the old Indian name "Micanopy" in 1834.

At the turn of the twentieth century, Mrs. Natalie Herlong arrived from South Carolina to inherit a parcel of land as well as a somewhat rundown large house in Micanopy. The Herlongs were forced to relocate from South Carolina to Florida because the family's business was failing terribly, and needing a home, the relocation seemed like a blessing. Mr. Herlong, however, never learned to love Micanopy as the others did, regretting the move from his beloved Carolina. Mrs. Herlong held the title to the property until she passed away, leaving the home to her six children. The only stipulation in the will, which was to be respected by the children, was that their father could live in the house for the rest of his life.

Mr. Herlong lived in the house another ten years until his death, leaving the six siblings in the rundown mansion. They all wanted the old Southern home, but only one of them could afford the expense: Inez Herlong-Miller. Inez was left a good amount of money when her husband, Fletcher Miller, died some years earlier. It was enough money, in fact, to buy out her remaining family, with enough left over to begin the much-needed repairs on the old house. Although the whole affair was legal and business-like, the family was exceedingly angry with Inez for buying the home for herself, and a family feud resulted when no resolution was found. The feud was so bad that the five siblings would never speak to Inez or enter the house again, thus leaving a painful rift within the Herlong family. Although Inez was adversely affected by the fighting, she was determined to restore the stately home to its original beauty with all the Southern charm it had had years before.

Inez was successful in restoring a good portion of the old farm-house in a beautiful and stately manner, reminiscent of the plantation homes of the nineteenth century. Nevertheless, although she was the victor in the family battle for the home, she had always regretted los-ing contact with her siblings and was even more distraught that the feud had caused so much bitterness and alienation. Sadly, the family home she fought so hard for and put so much time and effort into was not to remain a refuge for her in old age. Not long after Inez had taken control of the home, she passed away as a result of a heart attack while sitting in her sister Mae's childhood bedroom.

Today, the Herlong Mansion remains a beautiful example of his-torical architecture and timeless dignity. When you stay in one of the many rooms, you will get the relaxed feeling of old Florida, when life was far less stressful and without modern hassles. In this township, you can experience a small community mentality, where everyone knows each other and works together as a fellowship should. Although you won't find any bars or fast-food restaurants here, or giant multi-plex theaters or arcades, the city of Gainesville is only a few miles to the north, in case the peacefulness is just too peaceful for you.

As with all small towns, Micanopy has its own supernatural leg-ends, and it's no surprise that the Herlong Mansion is suspected to have a ghost residing within its stately halls and gorgeous bedrooms, as countless guests have told of their eerie experiences over the many years. Because Inez Herlong-Miller put so much effort and love into her family home, many believe it is her spirit who still finds refuge in the place she so loved in life. Although her spirit is hardly tormented, she maintains an almost constant vigil there, and her presence can almost always be detected in one way or another.

Ghostly Legends and Haunted Folklore

For the most part, Inez's spirit has a gentle nature, almost motherly. I have not personally heard or experienced anything negative about this entity, yet it is believed that those who have a dark or sinister nature will not enjoy their stay—cutting their visit short and fleeing before their scheduled stay is finished. Inez will not behave like the typical Hollywood ghost, jumping out at you or heaving objects; instead, an unfriendly visitor may have nightmares or experience bad feelings that will make him wish to abandon the bed and breakfast as soon as possible.

For most of us, however, a stay at the Herlong Mansion includes a deep, restful sleep. If you do experience anything out of the ordinary, it will most likely be of a whimsical nature, such as hearing strange noises or seeing the bedroom lights flicker on and off. Perhaps you will smell strange fragrances like flowers or perfume in the hallways, or spot foggy images in the corners of your eyes, but certainly nothing frightening. Although these are the most common phenomena witnessed, others have reported that when they awaken in the morning the overhead light will be on, and even stranger, the stereo that sits in the room will some times go on and off by its own accord. Moreover, as local legend tells, when you leave the bathtub half full overnight, strange things will happen. You may hear light splashing coming from the bathroom area, or hear echoes of a voice that cannot quite be made out. Sometimes the water will be completely drained in the morning, yet the plug will be set firmly in place.

Famed Gainesville-based parapsychologist and professor Dr. Andrew Nichols has conducted research at the Herlong Mansion over the years. His findings appear to indicate that the mansion falls into the category of the classic haunting, but as his field research is synonymous with tenacity, it's a good bet his inquiry there is not entirely finished. Other paranormal researchers, including myself, have stayed there in hopes of witnessing something out of the ordinary, and though the events are more of a subliminal nature rather than an out-and-out physical manifestation, some still claim to have experienced the fantastic.

My girlfriend and I stayed there in 2003, both for a romantic getaway as well as to accommodate our ghostly research. As she had stayed there before, she knew exactly which room to choose and where to go in town. When we got to our room, Inez's old room, she walked over to the dresser and picked up a diary. This book is placed there specifically so the guests may log their experiences while staying in the room. Going back through the years, hundreds of past guests have jotted down experiences ranging from a quiet night to downright spooky occurrences. After settling in, we enjoyed a lively night in downtown Gainesville, then returned to the Herlong for tea, then to bed for a well-deserved rest. While she stayed up most of the night, waiting for the extraordinary, I fell asleep and slept a deep, thoroughly restful sleep like I had not had since my childhood. In the late morning when we both awoke, we noticed that the headboard light was on, though neither she nor I had turned it on. Though this certainly does not constitute a major paranormal event, it does nonetheless make one take notice.

After having a wonderful breakfast in the parlor, we went to explore a little more before we had to depart for home. After looking around on all the floors, getting a feeling of what it must have been like in Inez's day, we finally ended up in the drawing room. Here, we found several videotapes of *Doc Hollywood* and *Cross Creek*, which were filmed in Micanopy, as well as another tape, which had no title. As the Herlong Mansion invites its guests to watch the television in the drawing room, we decided to have a look at this videotape. The video contained documentary-style footage of several men going underneath the Herlong Mansion, in what appeared to be a hidden chamber. Although no one is exactly sure what it was originally used for, many suspect it was a room used to isolate either slaves or servants when they angered their masters. Some have suggested it was used as a fruit cellar, but the location and layout is too bizarre for such use. Then there are some who believe that this room served another purpose as a secret occult meeting chamber.

The room below the mansion's foundation has very odd dimensions. Although it is difficult to discern the original diameter because of the erosion of the ground over the years, some believe that the original measurements were six feet wide, by six feet across, by six feet deep—an even 666! Regardless of the implications of this particular number, some to the contrary believe that the original measurements were more like 777, which sounds a good bit less threatening. Though this room remains something of a mystery to this day, many suspect that some form of mystic order may have held their meetings here many years ago, although there are no historical documents to prove its existence. Moreover, the video showed these urban explorers finding a tattered piece of paper, faded and aged, with either the words "help us" or "help me" written on it.

Although there have been no reported physical manifestations or apparitions of Inez, the sounds of doors slamming and footfalls on the second floor when there are no guests staying there add to the haunting enigma. Though rare, these events seem to have originated almost immediately after Inez's death. Apparently, when the mansion was purchased to be used as a bed and breakfast, the owners hired a Midwestern construction company to complete the work. Although Inez was able to begin the refurbishment of the mansion, her untimely death ceased her original plans. Fortunately, the new construction crew was able to understand Inez's wishes, and began work. During those days, there was no electricity in the house, so the workers could only work while there was sunlight shining in or by candlelight in the evening. The men had to sleep in the drawing room downstairs in order to get fresh air from the open windows. One evening, while they were just getting to sleep, they began to hear footsteps on the floor above them, pacing back and forth. Then they heard doors slamming, which naturally put them on alert, thinking that someone had broken in. As the men raced upstairs to seize the intruder, they found no one, not a soul. After the second night of this, the legend of the haunted Herlong house was born.

It seems that on occasion Inez will reenact this scene. Perhaps she wants to make a statement, or perhaps she's just playing games with the living. Either way, she is noticed. Events like these are indeed rare, and the most you can usually expect is a gentle feeling of being watched over, or the sound of water splashing in the bathtub. Perhaps a light will flicker, or the radio in your room will turn on by itself, and just maybe you will catch the gentle hint of perfume in the air. However, you will never feel threatened by the kind-hearted spirit of Inez, the Herlong Mansion's resident house mother.

Afterthoughts

We were sad when it was time to leave the beautiful Herlong Mansion Bed and Breakfast. Staying a night there was one of those experiences I will not easily forget—not for expensive champagne or caviar waiting in the rooms or fancy amenities we have come to expect in our fast-paced society. No, the Herlong Mansion was designed to cater to an older, more refined type of person who knows how to relax and appreciate the style and class of long ago. And if you are looking for a ghost, this should be your haunted destination as well.

The spirit of Inez Herlong is anything but scary, as she behaves more like a mother than anything frightening. When I slept in her room, my sleep was so peaceful that words cannot describe. It seemed as soon as I got into bed I knew I was staying in a good place, with the feeling I was being watched over by someone who truly cared for me. When we awoke to find the soft headboard light turned on above us, we both felt comforted regardless of the strangeness of such an event. It seemed as if we were being gently awakened so as not to miss breakfast.

This bed and breakfast does indeed appear to be haunted, as it has all the right attributes of a classic haunting. The presence of cold spots, floral scents, and flickering lights only add to this assessment, but more than anything supernatural, I would have to say the feeling of a presence stands out the most. Perhaps it's the child in all of us that remembers feeling safe when our parents assured us everything would be all right, despite our fear of the dark or the thunderstorm that raged outside. It's that feeling of reassurance one gets at the Herlong Mansion, as if Inez watches over all her guests.

When traveling north-central Florida, be sure to visit Gainesville. See the many sights this college town has to offer, but also take a few hours to stop by the charming little town of Micanopy. If you have some time set aside for a special occasion, spend a night or two at the Herlong Mansion—you'll be glad you did. Enjoy the gracious staff, delight in the charms of old Florida, and relax a bit. If you are fortunate enough to feel the presence of Inez, simply thank her for the opportunity to stay in the mansion she called home for the majority of her life . . . and apparently continues to do so today.

The Herlong Mansion is located at 402 N.E. Cholokka Boulevard in Micanopy, Florida, and may be reached at 352-466-3322.

4

Hotel Blanche

Lake City

So Much Unhappiness . . . So Much Unrest

*Some places are strange, that's no surprise, but this place
has something to it . . . something just not right. You'll know
this when you walk by it late at night . . . I guarantee it.*
—*Email response from a former security guard*

A Little History

The Hotel Blanche, simply known as "the Blanche" by many living in
the Lake City area, is one of north Florida's silent reminders of a different era. Located at 212 North Marion Street, this huge building
served as the cornerstone of Florida hospitality for many years. The
three-story brick hotel, designed by architects Frank Pierce Milburn
and Henry W. Otis, has an eclectic facade and occupies a whole city
block. It once served as Lake City's premiere hotel and the primary
social facility for much of the northern part of the state.

From 1902 to the 1950s, the Blanche was the seat of luxury in the
small township of Lake City, offering its refined amenities and fine
dining to locals and travelers alike, in addition to hosting parties and
social functions for those five decades. Over the years, however, the

Blanche would experience many hardships. Tight budgets, the Great Depression, and two world wars took their toll on most of the United States, but Florida was among the worst hit, and the Blanche felt the crunch. As time marched on and the state matured, small college towns like Gainesville, about fifty miles south, grew into destination cities and in the process, overshadowed smaller towns like Lake City. It was just a matter of time before the Blanche's charm and popularity waned. Today, the Hotel Blanche is not in service as a resort, and although there have been rumors of its rebirth, plans to restore to a working hotel have yet to be announced.

Although by 1949 the Blanche's vacationing clientele was dwindling, the hotel did carry on in other functions. In the later part of the 1950s right up to the 1970s, the Blanche's space was used for commerce and trade by private businesses and even specialty stores. Today, there are various government offices occupying the hotel, but the majority of the space remains vacant. The Hotel Blanche and its active past are no more than ghosts, just faint images of a once jubilant locale.

As with any lodging, there have been tragedies and sad occasions at the Hotel Blanche. Though the history is spotty in some respects (exact times and dates are a mystery), a few tragedies have been documented over time. In the over 100 years of the building's existence, we know that there was a least one murder that took place there, several deaths by natural causes, and one suicide. Finding the exact details to these events are close to impossible, so we have to rely on local legend and oral traditions to assist in retelling the supernatural stories that have come to be over the years. Even though there is a curious lack of hard evidence to support these tragedies, many of those renting space there, as well as the building's staff, have their own up-close and personal evidence. They all know that the old Hotel Blanche is haunted.

Ghostly Legends and Haunted Folklore

The Hotel Blanche is one of Florida's more obscure haunted places. Although there are a few who are fully aware of this haunted hotel, for the most part, it appears to be nothing more than an abandoned building. Many of the occupants, however, have had more than one paranormal experience. Since at least the 1960s, the Hotel Blanche has had a strange feel to it in one way or another. Most who have witnessed the many strange events that take place there all seem to feel the building is housing at least one spirit, but others feel there are many more.

Of the ghostly events, the most common things experienced are cold breezes passing through the hallways where there is no logical source of the draft, and many strange noises heard throughout the building. Most of the paranormal events seem to take place on the second and third floors, where the occupants have heard everything from clanking sounds—as if objects are falling off high places—to children running around and laughing, to disembodied footsteps echoing from the hallways. Many have witnessed doors opening and slamming shut by themselves, as well as lights turning on and off by unseen hands. Even more curious, there is a small hole on the second-floor ceiling, which appears to be getting larger by the day. This hole can be attributed to the natural event of the building decaying, a call for repair rather than exorcism, but everything from coins to old newspapers are said to have fallen out of this hole, for no logical reasons. Needless to say, this is one bizarre building.

Computers are reported to act strangely on the second floor—the screens go fuzzy or stop working altogether. Although this is more annoying than scary, no one has yet found a plausible explanation for this technical oddity. Moreover, several of the workers have heard the sounds of children running around on the third floor, as if playing. The sounds of muffled, child-like giggles have been heard echoing from the third floor as well, and when investigated, the hallway and rooms are always found empty. Indeed, although these sounds reflect the blissful nature of happy children playing, such noises echoing from the vacant upper rooms still seem to frighten those who hear them.

In addition to these peculiarities, when staff and other workers walk on the second floor, near or around the ladies room toward the northern side, several people have reported smelling odd, misplaced scents, such as vinegar, sulfur, and even vanilla. Other scents like those of food cooking will be detected there as well, even though the restaurant downstairs has long been closed. Although these events may seem more weird than frightening, the sounds of disembodied voices and a woman sobbing uncontrollably have many at the Blanche in total apprehension.

Strange voices heard echoing from the upper floors are mostly whispering and incorporeal conversations, as if there were people walking around and having a chat. Investigators looking into the matter always search in vain—no source for the noises has ever been found. However, on occasion, some have even reported hearing a woman shouting and crying, as if in great pain. Often accompanied by doors slamming, these reverberations have been attributed to the spirit of a woman who committed suicide many years ago. Although no one knows a definite date for this event, many feel she took her life sometime during the mid-1930s. The most tragic aspect to this story, however, is that this woman killed herself while she was pregnant—an act that some believe is the reason for the horrible wailing and lamentations.

Because there is so little known about this woman, and no one has been able to find such a story in Lake City's old newspapers, we only have speculation for why she took her life at the Blanche. Perhaps the father of the child was unwilling to care for it; perhaps he was a husband who ran out on the woman in her time of need. Although there are any number of possible reasons, we will most likely never know for sure. What is known is that the Hotel Blanche has a very sad specter here, and she appears to have much to say.

This tormented spirit has never been seen, only heard crying and sobbing, and her words are never completely made out, although some have claimed to hear her call out someone's name. Unfortunately, the name she gives can never be understood, only muffled words. On some occasions, the screams are so loud that people walking on the adjacent streets can hear her. Wondering if there is some tragic event taking place inside, several people passing by have made inquiries into the nature of these screams, and some have been said to go inside the Blanche demanding to help this tormented woman.

Though there appears to be a rather large collection of spirits residing within the Hotel Blanche that are somewhat docile, they have a definite ability to frighten the living. No one has claimed to have been injured by any of these spirits, but there was one incident that had a fire marshal take notice of the paranormal. Evidently, when the city fire marshal was making an inspection of the Blanche some time ago, he had a direct encounter with something unknown while descending the stairs to the hotel's basement. According to the shaken fire marshal, as he was nearing the bottom step, having trouble seeing (only some of the lights were working), he lost his footing and fell. And, although this sounds like an everyday mishap, the fire marshal made a statement that changed the everyday to the supernatural. As he was just about to step off the last step, he said he felt the grip of an unseen hand, which pulled him down toward the floor. Though he wasn't injured, the poor fire marshal was, needless to say, a bit unnerved.

To date, there is still no word on plans for the Blanche's return to splendor. Whether or not it will be refurbished and brought back to life remains to be seen, but if this old gem from Florida's past is to resurface as a functioning, updated hotel, we can expect to hear more from her gathering of noisy spirits.

Afterthoughts

Although the Hotel Blanche seems to enjoy its anonymity from the ever-probing ghost hunters and psychics, it's only a matter of time before the clamorous specters within will call it to their attention. A definite history of the Blanche is just as elusive and mysterious as the wailing woman on the upper floors or the unseen children playing throughout this creepy building.

The mysterious hole on the second floor that is said to produce strange, misplaced objects from time to time, appears to point to a somewhat rare paranormal event known as an "apport." The apport is believed to be a portal from one location to another, whereby some paranormal force or spirit will transfer an object, such as coins, paper, and so forth, to another location. Many of these events have been attributed to poltergeist phenomena. Is the Hotel Blanche haunted? Just ask the government employees working there, and if their testimony isn't enough, then find that spooked fire marshal who felt the cold, unseen grip of what he referred to as a ghost.

If you're planning to visit the Hotel Blanche, keep in mind that this is a working office complex now, and permission must be sought before investigating. The best place to experience the aforementioned phenomena is within the building itself, but several witnesses over the years have heard strange noises while sitting outside the Blanche late at night. Although a ghost hunter may need to acquire permission before investigating inside, many of the workers there have been open about the strange events, as many of them have experienced odd things within this unique hotel of Florida's past.

5

School Four

Jacksonville

Jacksonville's Haunted School of Yesteryear

With every breath the air grows stale
Deathly cold winds howl and wale
Raging thunder pounds like drums
When something wicked this way comes.
—*Old nursery rhyme painted on School Four's auditorium stage*

A Little History

At 1011 Peninsular Place—just off I-95 and near busy streets, small shopping centers, and cafés—stands a very spooky building. A historical landmark for sure, this colossal structure, simply known as School Four, resonates a feeling of dread and evil that has been a part of Jacksonville's oral tradition for many years, and has been called "the most haunted place in Jacksonville."

The original structure was a wood-frame schoolhouse, built in 1891 on the city's common ash heap. Then, by 1917, the structure had been slowly upgraded with huge brick wings spanning in various directions, costing over $250,000. It was called "Public School Number Four" for many years, and later renamed "Annie Lytle Public

School," after its former principal. But it remains as School Four, known more for its ghostly reputation than its educational and historical significance.

Sitting on the edge of Riverside Park, School Four remained a beautiful landmark until major road construction and the march of progress upset the quaint setting in the late 1950s. Still, students continued to come and go, and as they did, many legends circulated the halls, like at any school in America. Some stories, of course, were more frightening than others. Tales of monsters lurking under the massive building, or of disgruntled teachers and janitorial staff going on killing sprees, or even of cannibal principals eating fifth graders were common fodder for students attending classes at School No. 4. Sadly, by the 1960s—as other improvements were being made around the now bustling city of Jacksonville, and as the march of progress advanced—

the fate of this time-honored place of learning would become clear: the school had to close in order to make room for newer and more productive buildings with better locations.

Even after closing, though, School No. 4 rested on the banks of Riverside Park as a quaint reminder of a simpler time in American history, and continues to do so even today. Yet regardless of its noble rank among educational institutions, or of the scores of students who graduated here, it's the more sinister reputation of the building that has lingered in people's minds rather than its gift of knowledge and scholarly intent.

School Four is the focus of several time-honored folk tales of the Jacksonville area, and is an object of spooky legend with the local youth. Although illegal and dangerous to enter the old building, many youthful adventurers conquer their fears and accept the dare to explore the most haunted building in the city. And, although School Four has been a major rite of passage for many, the true danger is ignored, in spite of all the telltale signs.

To my knowledge, this decaying landmark has no history of homicide or suicide; however, according to local law enforcement, School Four is a problem, although not necessarily of the supernatural kind. The satanic symbols written in blood, the violent graffiti that adorns the walls, the remains of crudely designed altars, and even the remains of sacrificed animals should be evidence enough that this haunted location should be viewed from the outside . . . never from within.

Although this once glorious monument of historical architecture is no more than a decaying shell of its former grandeur, the hint of its once strong and pride-filled existence still shines through, although there is also a definite hint of creepiness that cannot go unnoticed.

Ghostly Legends and Haunted Folklore

I was fortunate enough to have interviewed several people who have actually been inside School Four, and each of them was more than happy to admit that he was frightened by not only what he had seen, but by what he had felt as well. Apparently, there is an active nightlife within School Four's rotting corridors and abandoned classrooms . . . the kind of nightlife most of us would rather avoid. You see, School Four seems to attract more than the illicit drug users and transients—it also attracts Satan worshipers.

It is believed that as early as the 1960s the old deserted hulk was being used by many of society's outcasts. Hippies once used it as a commune and artist retreat, and in the 1970s there was a large transient population living there, always keeping the police on their toes. In the 1980s, however, after years of disrepair, the building began to take on a more sinister feeling, as one of my informants expressed. It was during the eighties that many of Jacksonville's less-traditional youth began to take part in more nefarious activities, which may have altered or enhanced the already questionable atmosphere of School Four.

This tremendous building appears to house all of the classic aspects of a haunting. The people who have been through the structure have expressed an uncanny fear of the place, as if it were truly alive. One of my informants, a native of Jacksonville now living in Tampa, told me of his many adventures as a self-styled School Four investigator of the unknown. He describes the building as having many areas that were unnaturally cold, and that there were always the sounds of movement in places where there should be no movement, like within the furnace or around the archways and rafters of the main hallway. Also, there is said to be a constant beam of soft light, which shines from the ceiling to one particular area in an old classroom that is always cold.

The evidence of orb activity is certainly present in photographs taken both inside and outside the school; in fact, almost every photo

I have seen of School Four has a plethora of orbs in it. According to many Florida ghost hunters, this form of energy may be a result of several things—one being the natural vibrations emitting from the site itself, known as earth energies, and another being the active manifestations of disembodied spirits. Of the many other photographic anomalies that occur in pictures taken within the building is the evidence of a mist or haze on the film. My experiences with taking photos of School Four always result in one photo that turns out relatively clear but with a misty streak, and the next photo will come out almost completely black, or completely foggy, followed by another clear photo. Many reputedly haunted locations will cause this photographic effect, and School Four is certainly no exception.

The feeling of an unearthly presence in the building is almost always reported by practically everyone who goes into School Four, as if there were someone watching them from a distance. Sometimes, as one walks through the hallways, the sounds of footsteps can be heard directly behind, which naturally cut the visit short.

The sounds of scurrying feet under the massive staircase can sometimes be heard, as well as the sounds of whispers coming from the corners of a huge room. The most common feeling is always one of pure, unadulterated fear. Yes, the building is old and literally falling apart, and the spooky atmosphere might just add to the natural fear factor as it would with just about any old building, but there is something more going on at School Four . . . something evil.

If you walk around toward the back of the school, you will see two overgrown courtyards—the old bricks covered with ivy and mold, the iron fences and railings rusted and pitted away, and the once great doorways now boarded up with decaying lumber. In addition, if you walk in these courtyards at night, it is said that you can hear the faint echoes of a school teacher dictating to her students and the occasional giggles of children behaving as children do. It is also said that if your hear these innocent sounds of long ago, you may feel something brush up against you accompanied by a cold gust of air, as if the ghostly children were just let out for recess.

School Four legend also tells us that before the windows were boarded up, passersby would occasionally see the faces of children looking out. Sometimes, these youthful spirits are seen running and playing in the classrooms, then fading away into the building's dark recesses; other times these childlike specters are seen staring out with a fixed look to those who behold them. Sometimes, a flash of dull light would appear floating through the hallways, bobbing up and down in a playful manner, adding to the already strange legend of this creepy building.

Even though the stories have varied over the years as to how or why School Four would be haunted, the very fact that so many have seen, heard, or felt something out of the ordinary should raise some questions. However, the fact that there has been so much negativity routinely practiced within the rotting halls could explain many things. The ritual worship of Satan and other evil entities might just attract existing spirits in or around the general location of School Four, thus creating a kind of ghostly convention center, which is not too appealing considering the malevolent goals of those who were attracting these spirits.

Even though the history of School Four seems quaint, and for the most part harmless, with no evidence of foul play within its massive circumference, the common belief remains that there is definitely something here that is not quite right.

Afterthoughts

In retrospect, I can honestly say that I was a little spooked when I looked on this massive wreckage. Is School Four the most haunted place in Jacksonville? Probably not. Yet considering it has been a home for so much negativity over the years, many feel a paranormal darkness has fallen over the old landmark. As it served as a pathetic refuge for those individuals who practice rituals for the intent of evil, many feel such behavior may have either created an evil atmosphere or have attracted evil itself.

One possibility, and a popular belief with many parapsychologists and ghost hunters regarding the haunted phenomena here at School Four, is that over the years the repeated fear and even anger brought to the building from one person to the next may have caused an emotional residue effect. Like the fine grooves in a record album, traumatic events are played over and over again until they are disrupted. When someone enters this location, he might bring similar fears and other negative feelings, thus reinforcing those grooves and repeating the recording.

This theory—known as a residual haunting, or more appropriately "cell memory replay"—might explain why such events happen on various occasions in cyclical fashion, though some suspect a definite intelligence existing within the darkened recesses of this fascinating old structure.

Today, while School No. 4 still stands as a decaying pentacle of the historic district, her days are surely numbered, though the end may not come for some time yet. This unique historical landmark was originally scheduled to become a condominium in the near future, with most of the original structure to remain, but apparently such a project will have to wait. Though there are many reasons for this, I can't help but wonder how the ghosts here will respond if those or similar changes finally do take place.

6

Chelsea Courtyards Apartments

Jacksonville

The Legend of Apartment 40

Our warm and inviting apartment community surrounds
you with the quiet and comfortable feelings of home . . .
You'll feel the warmth from the moment you walk through
the stately columns and enter our beautifully landscaped
grounds . . . And, you won't ever want to leave.
—old brochure for Carriage House Apartments

A Little History

Chelsea Courtyards, formerly the Carriage House Apartments, located at 2260 University Boulevard North in Jacksonville, represents another location synonymous with Florida's lively, if not downright frightening ghost stories. Build in 1966, these apartments were beautifully designed to suit anyone from families to college students. It's complete with 3 pools, a clubhouse and even guest cottages for visitors, while all surrounded by lovely courtyards and quaint gardens. These apartments have been, and continue to be a benefit for many of Jacksonville's residents. And, apparently, as the old brochure once said, "...You won't ever want to leave," which seems to be the case for at

A sign for Carriage House Apartments before the complex became Chelsea Courtyards

least a few unseen residents believed to exist in one of the apartments.

Before the Carriage House Apartments became Chelsea Courtyards, the complex was a source of local ghostly legend dating back at least twenty-five years. The complex's ghost or ghosts, which one would assume remain despite the change in name, seem to revolve around apartment 40. According to the local legend, this apartment has been unlivable for years. Locked and used as a storage room for the maintenance crew, apartment 40 was said to have been shunned because the spirits within allow little rest to anyone living there. But, as legends go, many aspects of the stories that have been passed down from year to year have been altered, taking on new and improved qualities since the original telling. The Carriage House Apartments, not being immune to these rules, often led the ghost hunter down an unfortunate road of incorrect folklore, leaving them with nothing more than a spooky yearn. Such a mishap of oral tradition, telling more or less than the true ghostly tale, has given us the haunted enigma of apartment 40.

Ghostly Legends and Haunted Folklore

The story is as follows: Apartment 40 is very haunted . . . so much so, in fact, that no one has been able to live there for very long. Residents would be chased out by poltergeist activity, which is not only frightening, but also life-threatening, as objects could be thrown at the apartment dwellers, and blood has even been seen dripping down the walls. Plus, the scent of decaying flesh and ghostly, rotting faces seen in the bathroom mirrors are just some of the creepy tales associated with apartment 40. The legends continue to tell of a ghostly white cat often seen in the front courtyard, and the front office that appears to be haunted by a short, elderly lady who creates a pleasant, homey feeling there. Needless to say, stories like these will have any paranormal investigator rushing to do research.

As one of my fellow researchers and I were making a north Florida ghost-hunting expedition in early 2002, investigating some of Jacksonville's other fascinating haunts, we were expecting the unknown. With haunted places like the Casa Marina Hotel, the Homestead Restaurant, the very creepy School Four, and the W. J. King House of Mayport Village, it was only natural to stop by for a personal and up-close look at the then Carriage House Apartments. We did so, and got the facts about this legendary Florida haunting.

When we arrived that Saturday afternoon, we were impressed how nice this complex was, and yes, as the brochure stated, it did give off a safe and homey feeling. Before we set off to talk about the legends with the management, we drove around the complex to identify the locations spoken about so often on the Internet, in books, and in periodicals. We spotted the front office where the kindly ghost is said to exist, and the spacious courtyard behind the office where the disappearing white cat is believed to roam, and finally, the parking lot in front of the infamous apartment 40. As soon as we parked, an incredible thing took place: an elderly gentleman walked out of apartment

40, got into a late-model aqua-colored Ford, and drove off.

My friend and I looked at each other in surprise, as this apartment, which was reportedly locked up and no longer used as a dwelling for the living, was in fact a well-used apartment and had been for some time. This disrupted a favorite legend of ghost hunters all over the state and beyond. We decided to walk around and ask anyone if they knew about the haunting of apartment 40, and it wasn't long before we met an older lady walking her dog. When we politely asked about the haunted apartment, she nodded her head and smiled, as if she had heard that question many times before. The woman explained that the spooky history goes back many years, long before anyone died in there—if anyone ever had died in the apartment, she said. She continued to say that although apartment 40 has the reputation of being haunted, it is believed that that the apartment next to it is the real haunted one . . . apartment 42.

Naturally, this was a surprise to us as there were so many who have been led to believe that apartment 40 was the haunted one, that it was boarded up and shunned by anyone even walking past it. Now the myth was ruined, as apartment 40 is a well-used apartment, rented by a relatively happy and unfrightened elderly gentlemen. Very strange indeed.

The common story of the haunting tells us that an elderly couple lived in that apartment for many years, before finally being put in a nursing home and dying there in the late 1980s. Having loved the apartment so dearly, and considering it their home for many years before dying in the cold, medical environment of the nursing home, they may have decided to return to apartment 40 . . . or should I say, 42, as the case may be. Either way, even though this woman stated that she was a devout Christian and did not believe in such things, she was nevertheless fully familiar with the legend.

After this impromptu interview, we decided to walk up to the front office and ask a few questions. There we met a Mrs. Linda

Dunlap, the apartment complex's assistant manager. She was relatively open about the legendary ghosts of apartment 40 and said that many of those stories have been exaggerated greatly. But, there have been those who claimed to have heard voices and whispers coming from or near the apartment, usually starting just before dark and ending before sunrise. As it is on a side street, just opposite a large field with horses in it, one is bound to hear a lot of things, she said. She added it had been vacant for about a year prior to the current occupant moving in. Then I asked about the front office being haunted, and this time she appeared to be more of a believer, as she herself claimed that strange things have happened there from time to time.

Among the strange events, which include lights going on and off by themselves, the air conditioning thermostat will change its setting, and the light scent of perfume will oftentimes be detected. Some have also claimed to see the shape of a short woman walking around the office after hours when the lights are off. Although Mrs. Dunlap did not claim to have seen such a sight, there was a woman who, while walking past the office's front window late one evening, spotted a small shape inside walking past the desk. The outside floodlights shone just enough into the office, and the woman thought it was just the manager getting ready to go home for the night and didn't give it another thought . . . at least not until the next day. You see, the woman came into the office the following day in order to pay her rent. She made the comment that she had seen the manager or the assistant manager the night before walking around with the lights turned off. However, the manager told her she had left around five o'clock the previous evening, long before it was dark. Moreover, the assistant manager was on her vacation during that time, so it could not have been her. And considering both the manager and the assistant manager were relatively tall and slender, they really didn't match the description anyway. There was only one woman matching that description who had business in the office, and that was Billie Boyd. Although this could be a plausible explanation, there was only one problem—she's been dead since 1987!

The longtime staff as well as the longtime residents of the Carriage House Apartments all knew and loved Billie Boyd. She was the beloved mainstay of the apartment complex. If you had a problem, Mrs. Boyd would take care of it. Even if it was four o'clock in the morning and the shower ran cold water, she would look into it; or if the plumbing was out of service, the maintenance man would soon be knocking at the door to fix the problem. Billie Boyd not only took her job seriously, she really cared for the residents almost as if they were her own children, and everyone who lived there knew it.

Sadly, Billie Boyd died of cancer in 1987. It's not too terribly surprising that this spirit is Billie Boyd—as helpful and considerate as Billie was in life, it would be just like her to help out without getting in the way. If you forget to turn off the lights when you leave for the day, it's a good bet they will be turned off when you arrive in the morning; and if you forget to adjust the thermostat at night, don't worry, it's likely to be set to the right temperature in the morning. The spirit in the complex's office is a good one, and all the employees are happy to work there. As far as I know, there have been no complaints about the kindly ghost, and no one wants her to leave.

The ghostly cat that has been occasionally seen on the courtyard lawn has been described as an ordinary white cat that crouches close to the grass, and then simply vanishes when approached. This particular kind of haunting or manifestation seems to be somewhat common, and there have been many reports of phantom animals throughout history. Often thought of as foretellers either of doom or of good fortune, these particular apparitions remain very much unexplained. What particular purpose the Chelsea Courtyards cat serves is unknown, but apparently, some have witnessed the vanishing cat giving a look of fear or anger, always staring right at the witness as it simply turns to thin air.

Incidentally, not long after I finished this investigation, I heard from a friend who lives in Jacksonville that apartment 40 was vacant once again. Apparently, the elderly gentleman who had been living there when we visited was seen packing up his belongings in the middle of the night and driving off to an undisclosed location, not to return. Ghosts? Vacation? Family crisis? No one seemed to know for sure, and no one was talking. Even if there are no ghosts in apartment 40 or the other locations throughout the complex, there does seem to be something that's just not right there . . . something frightening.

Other possible explanations for the haunted phenomena include the Boys' Home located at 2354 University Boulevard North, just next door, a location that some believe to be the true source of the paranormal activity. It is believed that there is a banshee-like spirit residing there, and indeed, screams have been heard in the past, and the horses on the property have been seen running away from the apartment side of the field.

Even more strange is that when this banshee screams, a terrible event will usually soon follow, such as the murder or death of someone connected to the apartments. On one such occasion several years back, soon after a strange scream was heard in the night, a disturbed man went on a killing spree. He murdered his ex-girlfriend, and then his own wife, who lived in one of the Carriage House apartments . . . apartment number 42 to be exact. Although, thankfully, such things are not common at the complex, one can see why this legend has become at least a subject of speculation for many paranormal investigators today.

Afterthoughts

When I visited the complex now known as Chelsea Courtyards, I found it truly did resonate a down-home feeling, surrounded as it was by swaying canopy trees and complimented by a gentle breeze whistling through the corridors, and there did seem to be some kind of enchantment there. Does the gentle spirit of Mrs. Billie Boyd walk through those corridors at night, watching over the office and the people now working there even now? Are the legends of a poltergeist in apartments 40 and 42 true? And the disappearing phantom cat—are such things possible? Whether these ghost stories are indeed fact or just overactive imaginations creating good campfire spook stories, this apartment complex certainly has something more to it.

If you visit the Chelsea Courtyards Apartments, talk with the managers and ask to take a little walk around. See if apartment 40 is vacant, and if it is, try to hear the whispers coming from that apartment. Walk down the corridors that lead to the courtyard, past the office, and if you're lucky, maybe you'll see the elusive white cat melt away in front of you, or perhaps you too will see the shadowy shape of the ghost walking slowly through the darkened office.

One thing is for certain, a truly haunted location does not have to be a graveyard, a spooky, deserted old building, or a creepy old castle in England. Hauntings, poltergeists, and other paranormal activity can take place in relatively new apartment complexes such as Chelsea Courtyards, or in relatively new homes like yours or mine. Indeed, ghosts are not necessarily particular about their afterlife residences, nor are they necessarily particular about who they live with. Who knows, a spirit may want to live in your apartment or home . . . perhaps one already does!

7

Homestead Restaurant

Jacksonville

Some Ghosts Just Like to Hang Around

A Little History

Located just a few miles west of Jacksonville Beach at 1712 Beach Boulevard, the Homestead Restaurant sits, nestled amid Australian Pines and scrub jays. Known for its family-style dining and quaint, old-time atmosphere, the Homestead Restaurant has had a powerful impact on the local residents of Jacksonville and abroad since 1947. Chicken dinners are their specialty, from fried to fricassee and pot pie to their famous chicken and dumpling dinners. The Homestead has inspired and satisfied the hungry for years.

The Homestead is a two-story log cabin surrounded by a white picket fence, under an umbrella of cascading trees draped with Spanish moss. Now painted beige, with blue-green shutters, the restaurant has a homey charm that is inviting and humble, proclaiming it to be an All-American eatery that won't let you walk away hungry. This restaurant has served customers for years, feeding and entertaining locals and vacationers alike.

Unfortunately, when I conducted my investigation there in 2003, the old Homestead sat deserted and dirty, as if it had been abandoned

The Homestead as it appeared in 2003.

by its owners and staff in the night. The restaurant was a pale yellow then, adored with tattered awnings that seemed to say "Go away and leave me alone!" Indeed, the old Homestead Restaurant sat silently off the busy road, overgrown with trees and moss, the wood sidings covered in mold. Then, the Homestead appeared unlikely to return. There was speculation that the owners then hadn't paid their rent on time, or that the restaurant had failed the health code inspections, forcing it to close. Some suggested there was a lawsuit of some kind pending. Though the restaurant owners in the area I spoke to during my last visit did not know for sure what had happened, they all believed that the Homestead Restaurant was doomed. But it did return, and is now open again for a second time since 2005.

I first saw the Homestead Restaurant back in 1997 while visiting a friend in Jacksonville. It was indeed a homey restaurant. I remember I had fried chicken that night, along with mashed potatoes, green beans, and biscuits. I also remember that the large limestone fireplace was ablaze that night in early January. The fireplace was a nice addition to the ambiance, but I feel sure this restaurant will always be remembered for its home-style food. I recall that there was a particular feeling I got there, as if my mother and father, or grandmother were there, as if I were at a family get-together: just plain cozy and nice. Yet I knew something else was there, something underlying that I just could not put a name to.

Ghostly Legends and Haunted Folklore

The history of the restaurant is a little spotty, but most of the local residents report that the land and some of the building's structure were once home to an adoption agency, operated in the late 1880s by a widowed school teacher named Angle Rosenburg and her daughter, Annie. Then, in 1934, the log cabin we see today was built by Alpha Paynter, a somewhat eccentric local luminary who turned the building into a boarding house for the local workers and seamen of a bustling Jacksonville. Later, in the 1940s, Paynter expanded her boarding house to a restaurant, which was a successful and popular venture right up to the late 1990s. Paynter died in the 1960s, and was laid to rest in the backyard of her beloved boarding house, restaurant, and home.

The Homestead had several owners in the years after Paynter's death, all of whom managed to keep its happy and hearty reputation until those last few years before the restaurant closed, when customers complained that the service had declined and the atmosphere became less than homey. The restaurant's esteem finally seemed to run out, at least until new owners took over and restored the place to its former glory. Yet, through the thick and the thin, from one plate of chicken and dumplings to the next, the ghostly legends have continued, so it might just be that the spirits of two hanged women and an old eccentric woman do indeed echo through the halls of the Homestead Restaurant.

The most popular spirit of the Homestead Restaurant is that of Alpha Paynter, the old boarding house operator. In life she was very attentive to her customers in the 1930s, and continued her hospitality right up to the day she died on December 8, 1962, at the ripe old age of 75. Alpha so loved the old log cabin that she arranged to be buried in the backyard, just before the woods, under an old tree. The grave is still there, of course, but it's now covered by a large bush and overgrown grass, its marker a victim of age and weathering. But, if you walk straight from the cabin's rear kitchen door and look hard enough, just to the left of the property, you may find what's left of Alpha's grave.

In her day, it was common to use the big limestone fireplace as the main source of heat during the winter. She would sit in a rocking chair by the hearth in order to stay warm, and she would often read by the light of the fire and fall asleep there when waiting for her boarders to come home for the night. She was said to worry about her clientele, enough to stay up and make sure they got home safely, which may be the reason her ghost has often been seen standing by the fireplace on cold nights.

Over the years, restaurant staff members have reported seeing the apparition on the first floor standing right next to the fireplace, looking toward the front entrance. She was seen by the bartender there one evening in the early 1990s walking slowly in front of the fireplace, then looking directly at him only to fade right before his eyes. The bartender suddenly began believing in ghosts.

Other employees have claimed to see what appeared to be an elderly woman walking up the stairs, holding her dress up slightly to avoid tripping on it, and not responding to the employees' questioning. As the upstairs portion of the cabin is now an office and storage area, it was odd that someone would just stroll up there. When the staff followed the elderly lady upstairs to see why she was going to an obviously restricted area, she was never found, but the air was apparently very thin and charged with electricity, as if on a high mountain. Strange events to be sure, but this spirit seems to stay away from the action of the living and focuses on inspecting her old homestead . . . just making sure everything's in place and just right. Now, no one can say for sure if Alpha Paynter's spirit is happy that the living have departed, but it's probably safe to assume that she's still checking up on things, and most likely residing by her beloved fireplace.

Although the gentle presence of Alpha Paynter is nothing less than your classic haunting and certainly no more a threat than the accumulated dust and cobwebs that now dominate the abandoned eatery, the presence of two other, more disturbed entities seems to prove a darker side of the building's haunting. These two sad spirits are believed to be those of Angle Rosenburg and daughter Annie Rosenburg. Apparently, the cabin built in 1934 was once used as an adoption agency during and immediately after the Civil War. Angle Rosenburg was said to be a loving, hardworking widow who devoted her life to the placement of abandoned, neglected, or orphaned children. She was also said to be a sad woman, however, who most likely suffered from depression or similar mental illness. Sadly, her daughter also suffered from this same condition. In a time when there was little to no help for such illnesses, most of those who suffered either lived with their afflictions, locked up in their homes or in an asylum, or ended their own suffering. Perhaps mental illness was hereditary in their family, or perhaps the losses resulting from the Civil War were just too much to bear. But whatever the reason, there is an obvious sadness at the Homestead that continues beyond the grave.

The facts about these two women are somewhat lacking. Even though evidence for the existence of a Miss Angle Rosenburg can be found in the city's archives from the 1860s, word of the two suicides can only be found in the local oral traditions. Indeed, the stories about the spirits of these two women have been told and retold by the Homestead's staff over the years. No one knows exactly why Angle Rosenburg took her own life by hanging herself in a back room, or why nothing more was ever said about it. Still, many are just as baffled as to why her daughter Annie did the same exact thing in a storage closet ten years later. Why was there so much sadness for them and why is their history so elusive? Were the Rosenburgs real people, or just victims of a misconceived legend? Only the former staff and at least one patron would know for sure.

There is said to have been one visitor to the restaurant in 1999 who claimed to have a shocking experience in the ladies' room. Evidently, a teenage girl, after enjoying one of the Homestead's famous chicken dinners, excused herself and headed for the ladies' room. While washing her hands, she is said to have seen the reflection of what she believed to be the apparition of a middle-aged woman in the mirror, a woman as white as a sheet and with large eyes staring right at her! When the girl turned around to see who or what was standing there, she saw nothing, only an empty bathroom. When she turned to look back at the mirror, the pale woman was still there, and, according to the legend, the ghostly woman asked the teenage girl to "Enjoy what you're doing and take care of those around you." The girl then shrieked, as I think anyone would have, and ran out of the restroom only to have everyone staring at her as if she were out of her mind. When she gave one of the employees a desperate look, the employee asked her if she had seen an old woman in the bathroom who told her to enjoy what she was doing and to help others in life. Obviously, it wasn't the first time something like this had happened. Apparently, this ghost made a habit of making sure everyone was as attentive and kind as she had striven to be in life.

The daughter, Annie, is said to have made a few visits as well. She has been seen in the backyard looking toward the ground, and in one of the old rooms upstairs, sitting in a chair by the window and holding her head in her hands, as if deep in sorrow. She is described as around the age of eighteen, twenty at the most, dressed in a black dress with a white collar. Strangely, almost nothing is known about Annie beyond the speculation of a few employees and even fewer Jacksonville residents.

Whether the legends of the Rosenburgs are nothing more than the elements of an overactive imagination, or actual tormented spirits cursed to repeat the unhappy events of an unhappy life, we may never know. Now that the Homestead is open once more, we may in fact learn the truth about the haunted nature of this location. After all, ghost hunters everywhere again have the chance to be welcomed by Alpha Paynter, or even to hear the heartfelt advice of Angle Rosenburg . . . but only if we're lucky.

Afterthoughts

For the traveling ghost hunter, the Homestead Restaurant is a must-see while in the Jacksonville area, and for sure, if you stop by for a look, take the time to just sit in your car for a long look at the upstairs windows. If you look into those darkened windows after the restaurant has closed for the night, maybe you too will get a glimpse of the young, sad Annie Rosenburg sitting there in her eternal misery. She might even look back at you with those sad eyes in an effort to explain her torment. And if you go in for a meal, look long and hard at the fireplace. Maybe you'll see the hazy vision of the ever-welcoming Alpha Paynter, and perhaps she will welcome you to stay in her boarding house. If you're lucky enough to visit the upstairs rooms, maybe you'll see the silhouette of Mother Rosenburg hanging from the rafters, as a reminder not to be too hasty in times of sadness and depression.

The Homestead is and shall remain a landmark of haunted legend for all Florida ghost hunters and paranormal investigators, regardless of its future. When visiting the restaurant, enjoy the laid-back atmosphere and especially the excellent food, which seems customary for this location. During the daylight hours, see if you too can figure out what Annie Rosenburg is looking for in the backyard, and whether you can find the long, forgotten grave of her long-dead mother. Then later, after the restaurant closes, be sure to keep an eye open for the spirited residents that have been dead for many years. For sure, this is one of Florida's best haunted locations, and should be on your list when exploring Florida's northeastern coast.

The Homestead Restaurant is located at 1712 Beach Blvd., Jacksonville Beach, FL 32250. For more information, call: 904-247-6820, or visit: www.homesteadrestaurant.us.

8
Casa Marina Hotel
Jacksonville

Haunted Hollywood's Summer Home

Some seem to think that there are these spirits, the sometime playful, sometimes frightening souls that still reside at the Casa Marina, still making it their home after all these years.
—H. Smyth Jr., Jacksonville Resident

A Little History

When visiting Jacksonville's beaches, you can't help but notice the beautiful beige, Spanish-style hotel that silently sits, embracing the ocean as if for its own pleasure. Holding north Florida's unique history deep within its halls, the Casa Marina Hotel, located at 691 North First Street, is one of those places that resonates a stately class in every sense of the word. Without the need to flash its charms as many of the beachfront hotels do, the Casa Marina has its own special allure. Its grand opening in June of 1925 was the same day that Pablo Beach was renamed Jacksonville Beach, in accordance with a popular vote. Jacksonville was truly a boomtown then, as Henry Flagler was gracing all Floridians with his unique and artful architecture, building his masterpieces all across the Sunshine State. The land and train barons

were mapping the new city, and even Hollywood stars and starlets took part in Jacksonville's new opportunities, including the relatively slow-paced atmosphere that Florida's north coast had back then. The hotel stood in all its glory even during World War II as it served as military housing for our soldiers and sailors. Then, as times changed, the hotel was converted into an apartment complex in 1983 with several stores and a restaurant downstairs. Then came financial problems, which forced the stately hotel finally to close in 1987. The building sat boarded up and abandoned until 1991, when a couple from Atlanta purchased the old hotel and slowly nursed it back to its original glory.

Today, after much effort and love was put into the restoration of this beautiful hotel, the Casa Marina once again holds that special charm that has not been seen in many years. When enjoying one of the Casa Marina's classy dinners or having a cocktail on the large patio, cooled by the fresh sea air, you'll realize why it was once a popular playground for many of America's elite.

Although we might think of Jacksonville as a relatively quiet place in the 1920s, when the beaches were still free of homes and condominiums and the population was sparse at best, the Casa Marina Hotel had an elegant reputation to it, even back then. Attracting the wealthy crowd in particular, the Casa Marina ultimately became a hot spot for many of Hollywood's vacationers. With hopes of transforming Florida's northeastern coast into a "little Hollywood," many actors, producers, directors, and their film crews found Jacksonville and the surrounding areas of particular interest. The wilderness, the beaches, and the frontier that Florida was back then made everything look picture perfect, and the nightlife and seamlessly endless parties that the Casa Marina hosted were appealing, too. These parties were so popular, people would've given anything to attend . . . some people even gave up the ghost.

Ghostly Legends and Haunted Folklore

On a recent visit to the Casa Marina, in hopes of finding a good story on a dark and rainy Saturday night, I sat in the hotel's bar having a nice conversation with the bartender and learned a few points about the hotel's illustrious past. That past may be just as active today, as apparently there are a few ghostly entities that refuse to depart this charming hotel. Evidently, these entities can be heard stumbling and shuffling around in one of the upstairs deluxe suites, and a portly gray shadowy figure has occasionally been seen on the southern staircase. In addition, there is an unseen presence that has been known to trip people while they near the seventh stop on the main staircase—a paranormal event that seems to be as old as the hotel.

Hearing that the Casa Marina had a few ghosts was my invitation to do a little research, hoping to find the identity of at least one of these ghostly entities. While interviewing several of the employees there, I found that among the Hollywood personalities that stayed and partied during the Roaring Twenties were such notables as Jean Harlow, Mary Pickford, Buster Keaton, and Fatty Arbuckle. There were famous musicians, artists, and the land and train barons that were working so diligently on making Florida a major presence in the United States. The Casa Marina was quite the place to be. As there were unhappy endings for many of those Hollywood legends of years past, it stands to reason that these restless souls just might wish to relive the better times, over and over again. And apparently, some of them do just that.

My research brought me to interview Mr. Harry Smyth Jr., a life-long resident of Jacksonville, who remembered the Casa Marina during its golden age, when it was a military barracks, when it stood abandoned, and when it was brought back to life in the 1990s. Mr. Smyth also remembered those wild parties, when the champagne flowed and the sounds of laughter echoed from the verandas and the beachside patio. He remembered when the silent movie actor and comedian Fatty Arbuckle stayed at the Casa Marina, the sad controversy of Fatty's fall from Hollywood's grace, and even the rumors of his ghost being seen walking on the boardwalk behind the hotel at night. Needless to say, when I heard that last part of Mr. Smyth's memories, I was compelled to dig a little deeper.

There are few of us today who can remember Fatty Arbuckle and the scandal that forced his decline in the early 1920s. When we look at his past, he was certainly a prime candidate for becoming a tormented spirit in the future. At the time, it was the worst scandal in Hollywood's history. As the story goes, in 1921, Roscoe "Fatty" Arbuckle, was accused of raping and murdering Hollywood-hopeful Virginia Rappe during a wild party in a posh Hollywood hotel. Although he was acquitted of those charges, Fatty Arbuckle was ostracized, ridiculed, and essentially exiled from Hollywood, and as a result, his sadness and depression became equally legendary. Even though his friends, like Buster Keaton, got him bit parts in acting and directing, Fatty never really got the chance to make it back to the glory he once had.

Fatty Arbuckle, trying to get his life back in order, did a lot of traveling. He traveled all over the world, and according to the hotel's records and journals, he made a stop or two to the Casa Marina Hotel in hopes of working with directors in what was becoming known as "Little Hollywood." Although the Casa Marina played a role of temporary happiness for the once Hollywood great, he never quite recovered from the scandal. He was a shy, quiet man now, reserved and distant.

He would walk on the old boardwalk near the hotel alone and look off at the waves pensively, as if looking for absolution. Moreover, although he was able to laugh and clown around at parties, and play a round of golf with the producers and directors, he was never the same jesting man he once was. Sadly, after returning to Hollywood in 1933, just as his luck seemed to be returning, Fatty had a massive heart attack and died. He had recently gotten remarried and just signed to do a new film.

Most of the staff know of the spooky events that take place after hours and during the early morning in the hotel, and many claim to have had a personal incident or two as well. Some claim to have heard disembodied voices on the second floor, and even more commonly, some claim to have been tripped while ascending the main staircase, always on the seventh step. There are reports of a shape or shadow resembling a portly man seen near the southern stairwell, as well as reports of the scent of cigars and sometimes an odd-smelling perfume where there should be no such scents. Some have claimed to see the shadow of a man walking on the boardwalk behind the hotel at dusk, and on occasion, the same shadow may be seen passing by one of the penthouse windows when no one is occupying those rooms.

Now no one has suggested that this spirit is that of Fatty Arbuckle. But he was fond of the Casa Marina, as there he was able to distance himself from some of the pain and embarrassment of those earlier years. He was said to love Jacksonville and had hoped to work there with a clean start. But with those dreams cut short just as he was gaining ground, perhaps a residual of Fatty's strong emotions found those attributes of the Casa Marina a safe and happy place. Perhaps the dark figure on the boardwalk or in the window looking down at the sea is indeed that of funnyman Fatty Arbuckle. Perhaps he is the trickster tripping the guests going upstairs after the party has ended for the evening. Almost everyone who has looked through the registry at all the famous guests who stayed and played at the hotel feels that these supernatural occurrences must be the gentle, sometimes playful, sometimes frightening spirit of yesteryear's most popular comedian, Roscoe "Fatty" Arbuckle.

Incidentally, while a friend and I were having that drink and listening to the bartender talk of the hotel's wonderful past, a few strange occurrences took place. It was strangely quiet that night and the bartender, my friend, and I were the only people in the bar area, and the bartender was the only female in that part of the hotel. As my friend and the bartender were exchanging opinions about the alleged spirits of the hotel, I went to do a little exploring. I walked up the stairs where the phantom hand is said to trip patrons going to their rooms for the night, and when I reached the seventh step, I was extra aware of my footing on the stairs. As I lifted my leg over the step, knowing full well of what I was doing, I felt what seemed to be a strain on my foot, as if I were lifting my leg out of water. I looked to see if there was a lip on the step, which could be responsible for people tripping, but there was nothing.

After a moment, I looked around to see if the carpet was sticky, or if it had any holes in it that could be causing the effect—no problems there either. So, feeling a little stumped, I returned to the bar and took my seat. As I sat down, my friend turned to me and said that he could smell an odd perfume, although the bartender was away tending to the restaurant. Neither the bartender nor my companion was wearing perfume, and there was no one else in the bar at that time. My friend said that he felt his head begin to spin, as if there were a pressure change taking place in the bar just before he smelled the strange perfume. Paranormal investigators may look at this as a sign of a "portal haunting," wherein an ethereal door opens and closes, creating a kind of pressure change that can be felt especially in sensitive people. We can at least entertain such possibilities.

As my investigation continued, my friend and I walked around inside the old hotel and took some snapshots, then walked outside to do the same. As the rain had finally resided and the air was now crisp and relatively dry, I began to take a series of photographs, one after the other. I took photos of the walls of the building from many angles, in hopes of catching something out of the ordinary. When I was finished, we returned to our rooms for the evening, but it was not until the photos came back that we discovered a few interesting developments. Apparently, if we take the enigma of orbs to heart as evidence of a haunting, then the Casa Marina certainly has its share of ghosts.

The photos of the Casa Marina's orbs I took that dark night, although suspected to be nothing more than specks of dust or a raindrop caught on the lens, may be legitimate supernatural phenomena. Many still believe that these slightly iridescent balls are the disembodied souls of the dead, a kind of transportation system for the soul that many parapsychologist's claim is the easiest way for a spirit to get around. You can decide for yourself.

Afterthoughts

The Casa Marina is just one of those hotels that appeals to those who can appreciate the simpler, more thoughtful aspects of an older hotel. The beaches, the boardwalk, and the fresh salt air are the surroundings, and the hotel's inner delights revolve around a mature, classy atmosphere instead of a fast-paced, computer-age theme. Is the Casa Marina haunted? As with almost any area or location on earth, I would say yes. I say this because I believe, as many others do, that the ethereal plane, or spirit world, co-exists with our everyday reality.

Perhaps we just do not see this ghostly stratum or the entities that inhabit it as easily as self-proclaimed psychics might. Because most of us are logical people with more mundane things to worry about, with business and the daily grind to deal with, there is little time to think about ghosts and goblins. But consider this, haven't we on one occasion or another seen a baby looking into thin air, giggling away at absolutely nothing, for absolutely no reason? Or watched a dog or cat acting in a similar manner by barking or hissing at nothingness? What do they see that we cannot? Perhaps it's just a coincidence, or perhaps they are indeed seeing what we simply refuse to see, or can no longer see.

The next time you visit the Casa Marina, take the time to feel out that location. Walk up the stairs and through the quiet halls. Take the time to really look around and feel the surroundings, and perhaps you too will smell a strange perfume that has not been used for seventy years or so. Maybe you will see a foggy shadow climbing the staircase, or even feel a cold hand clutching your ankle as you ascend the stairs. Perhaps you will say it's only your imagination when you see the shape in the window while walking on the beach, or that you're just plain clumsy because you tripped on the seventh step. Just remember the lives lived at the Casa Marina, and the lives lost there, too. And remember Fatty Arbuckle, the comedian who died sad and ostracized from the life he loved.

9

Mayport Village

Mayport

A Gaggle of Ghosts in an Ancient Fishing Village

A Little History

Mayport Village, officially founded in 1562 as a seaport, is now a modern fishing hamlet and a truly notable location for Florida historians. Mayport now serves as the headquarters for the Marine Science Education Center, as well as home of the Mayport Naval Base, and this village should be on everyone's agenda when visiting northeastern Florida. Located just northeast of Jacksonville and Atlantic Beach, and nestled between Fort George Island and Amelia Island, Mayport Village has a unique feeling of ancient and adventurous sea history that should not be missed.

America's Timucuan Indians once thrived there and throughout most of this area for centuries. The area was later settled by the French Huguenots in the mid-sixteenth century, opening new growth and settlement to Florida's northern shores. Because Mayport and Fort George Island sit at the mouth of the St. Johns River, the area also became the stalking grounds for many of history's notorious pirates, buccaneers, and other disruptive naval forces for many years, right up to the American Civil War.

Mayport's history is actually quite intriguing, but it should also be known for its modern contributions to our country's defenses, which include the United States Naval Fleet Training Center, where sailors have been taught everything from propulsion plant operations to undersea combat since 1966. Mayport also houses a U.S. Coast Guard recovery and rescue base that is always ready to launch at a moment's notice. And for many of Mayport's residents, there are deep-sea fishing boats and offshore casino cruises that offer a relaxing atmosphere for Florida's sport- and ocean-loving folks.

With all the events that have taken place at Mayport Village over the centuries, it stands to reason that there would be a definite spiritual residue left behind—a residue of all those tragic wars, the pirate attacks, the Indian battles, and the conquest for land, that left thousands upon thousands dead. So perhaps many of those who died over this long period of time may not have left this earth satisfied or content . . . perhaps they didn't leave this earth at all. Perhaps many of those unfortunate victims of war and sickness over the centuries still roam Mayport Village. It is possible that when the sun goes down and the fog rolls in, so do the tortured souls that once inhabited this ancient land. Perhaps these spirits just head over to the old John King House on Ocean Street for the evening.

John King was one of Mayport's more colorful characters for many years, as many of the older folks recall. He had a reputation for telling ghost stories to the local children—stories of haunted houses and graveyards and things that go bump in the night, and stories of the sometimes playful, sometimes frightening ghosts and wandering spirits in his very own home. Moreover, although Mr. King is no longer with us, he has managed to pass his delightful legends on, and his stories resonate on into the wee hours, even to this day.

Ghostly Legends and Haunted Folklore

The John King House, built in 1881, is said to be one of the most haunted houses in Florida, probably because it may have more than one ghost living there, or maybe because so many people have had ghostly experiences within its walls. One thing is for sure, however: the old house was built directly on top of an old Spanish burial ground, and the bodies there were never recovered or relocated. Although John King lived in the house until his death in the 1970s, he apparently did not take the ghosts with him when he crossed over. Perhaps John King himself is still there, along with his friends.

There are paranormal echoes in the house, strange happenings of which many of the locals are aware. And because of the countless events reported, many psychics have visited the old house. These psychics speak of the many vibrant and unique ghosts there, though some of the spirits are more frightening than others. Moreover, the famous Rhine Institute of Duke University visited the location for the purpose of its own psychic and paranormal research, allegedly stating that the King house did indeed have both the right atmosphere for the classic haunting as well as a definite presence.

Of the notable spirits within the King house, one of my personal favorites is the ghostly butler. This petite man, who is dressed in a maroon-colored uniform, is said to open the front door for unaware visitors, then to direct them to the living room until the master of the house arrives. In John King's storytelling heyday, there were several such occasions when these events actually took place, to the delight of the jovial storyteller. However, no one has identified who the "little butler" could have been in life, though his costume is said to resemble those from the 1920s or 1930s. The little butler has been reported walking up and down the streets from time to time, and on some occasions, someone driving past will see the little man through the rear-view mirror, sitting solemnly in the backseat of the car. Naturally the driver pulls off the road in an understandable fit of fright, only to find his backseat completely empty. Who was the little butler who seems to have been one of Mayport's congenial gentlemen of a more civilized time?

Another legend tells of the haunted rocking chair, which is said to rock by itself when you stare at it . . . but who is doing the rocking? John King knew. Apparently, a relative of Mr. King, one of his aunts to be exact, was brutally murdered by an angry lover while sitting in the old rocker—actually stabbed to death with a pitchfork! Naturally a disgruntled spirit should emerge from such a violent act, and indeed, this women's tormented ghost is said still to walk down the corridors and creep around the bedrooms in the wee hours of the morning. Yet this spirit is more a prankster than a malevolent force. Pulling the bed sheets off while you sleep, opening and shutting doors right before your eyes, or turning lights on and off—it's that sort of poltergeist-like foolishness that this spirit is believed to cause, certainly nothing dangerous.

Although the rocking chair ghost seems to perform harmless acts of almost childlike behavior, there is another spirit who resides in the kitchen and is said to be the tragic result of an car accident years ago just outside the front doors of the King house. In this case, it is a tormented, yet eager-to-please spirit.

This ghost, known as the "lady in white," is thought to be that of a woman killed in that auto accident so many years ago, who then wandered into the old King house shortly after her death. At first, only the sound of echoing cries was heard, but then John King himself claimed not only to have heard these sad lamentations, but also to have seen this tormented spirit in his kitchen. Apparently, the sad, yet gentle woman was accustomed to continuing her chores, and so she does them as she might have done in life, wishing perhaps to be the perfect, loving wife she never got to be. You see, see died on her wedding night.

Although this is a rather sad tale of love lost, this spirit has apparently found a place to serve in the King house as a ghostly maid and keeper of the kitchen. Several people over the years claimed to have seen the lady in white over the kitchen stove, sweeping the dirt off the floor, or moving objects around throughout the house. The only negative aspect to this particular entity is that she is somewhat unpleasant to other females in "her" kitchen, and she has been blamed for many minor mishaps when other living ladies were visiting or using the kitchen.

Although the King house is a fine home, with a rather interesting gaggle of ghosts to say the least, I should also mention that there appear to be several phantom ships that cruise the waters around the jetties and inlets of Mayport Village. One of these ships is said to be a clipper ship with tattered sails snapping in the wind and no crew on her deck. This ghostly hulk silently glides through rough waters as if looking for a safe harbor. A second ship, which looks like an old-style fishing vessel, has been seen around these waters and nearby beaches, too, from Fernandina Beach to Atlantic Beach, always appearing to be in need of assistance. This ship is usually seen on foggy, moonless nights, or when storm winds blow and the waters are high, when the sea mist makes it nearly impossible to see. When the weather is just right, the dim beacons of this phantom vessel alert the locals that a fellow seaman is in danger, thus setting into motion a quick response from either the Coast Guard or even the U.S. Navy.

As late as 2000, the Navy was alerted to a vessel in possible distress and launched a rescue ship to its aid, only to find empty sea and no remains of a sunken ship. What makes this even stranger is that the ship that appears from time to time has been seen on radar blinking on and off, in the same rhythm as the phantom ship's blinking beacons, as if the ship itself were fading from this reality to another. In addition to this ghostly phenomenon, one of the Navy's own ships in

Mayport has its own ghost story to tell.

This particular ghost, known as "George," although completely harmless, has frightened even the heartiest of sailors. George is said to reside on the carrier USS *Forrestal,* deep in the hold of this massive ship. George has been heard walking up and down the lower levels and seen walking through an area that was once used as the morgue during the Vietnam conflict. He likes to open locked doors (which, incidentally, the Navy does not appreciate) and play with the lights from time to time. On occasion in the dead of night, a phantom telephone call will sound from a disconnected or non-functioning phone on an unoccupied lower level of the ship.

The sight of a sailor walking around is the most common experience, and when an investigation takes place, the sailors doing the investigation find nothing outside of a cold, spooky room. Many of the sailors ask who George may have been in life, but unfortunately, that is a hard question to answer, as so many have died in the heat of combat. One popular guess is that George may have been a chief petty officer who was killed by a fire in 1967 that killed more than 130 sailors. Some believe that he was one of the dead crewmen who were stored in these lower compartments when they were used as a sickbay and morgue. Either way, the USS *Forrestal* is haunted and the sailors know it.

Afterthoughts

When visiting Mayport Village, try to remember how ancient this little hamlet truly is, and try to remember the extensive history that took place there—the countless ships lost at sea in and around the waters of Mayport, the countless lives lost during the growth of our now thoroughly modern Florida. Try to remember that before it was the modern town it is today, it was a home to unspeakable violence and war. When driving down Ocean Street in the dead of night, when it's foggy or raining, try to keep an eye out for the little man dressed in the maroon uniform walking alone in the dark. Look toward the waters of the jetty or Ribault Bay for the phantom ship as it passes by within a veil of ghostly ether.

10

Sunland Hospital North

Tallahassee

In Memoriam:
The Final Days of Florida's Hospital of Horror

Sunland is not a place that takes kindly to strangers. When it became a hospital, it was one of the first to use electro-shock therapy in the area. A chrome tub, with a small amount of water, was a torture device for many of the patients, where they received jolts of electricity to curb their fits. The pit was a place where they were herded and left, screaming and laughing, because these patients were considered psychotic and deranged individuals.
They were left there for days.
—Anonymous ex-employee

A Little History

If there is one location in the state of Florida that elicited equal parts dread and excitement in people—with just the right amount of psychic impressions of regret and destitution, and finally culminating in a nefarious notoriety—it's the late Sunland Hospital in Tallahassee. Originally a noble and active hospital within a chain of caring, state-of-the-art hospitals, it would decline to a place of great disappointment and impiety, and in the end, would even harbor a reputation of pure evil.

This particular Sunland Hospital, also referred to as "Sunnyland" by many Florida ghost hunters and psychical researchers, was one of the most mysterious and downright formidable locations for anyone interested in ghost lore and the supernatural. And indeed, Sunland's demolition in 2006 marks the end of a time-honored tradition of ghostly legends and haunted folklore that had inspired Florida researchers for decades. Since its closing and abandonment in 1983, the hospital's massive decaying hulk, which ended up sitting virtually forgotten and shunned for more than 20 years, had taken on an almost unhealthy feel to it, as if it just did not want to die.

Sunland Hospital had an interesting beginning to say the least, and there were once several now defunct hospitals with the name Sunland. The first structure was built in 1921 in Gainesville, Florida, and was called the Florida Farm Colony for the Epileptic and Feeble-Minded before becoming a Sunland Hospital. The facility is now a community for the developmentally disabled called Tacachale, operated by the Department of Children and Families. In the 1930s, a Sunland facility in Pine Hills, Florida, was constructed as a tuberculosis center, and later housed those with mental disabilities.

The Tallahassee Sunland, located in Leon County, became an object of much controversy that continues to this day. Construction of this hospital began in the summer of 1950, and it was a jewel for the medical profession and the state itself. It cost close to $4 million to complete, and held over 400 beds. By 1954 this hospital served as a testing center for tuberculosis, and was known as the W.T. Edwards Tuberculosis Hospital.

By the late 1960s the hospital underwent an internal change, had a well needed facelift, and then adopted the name of the now infamous Sunland Hospital for mentally disabled children. This happened when eighteen disabled children from central Florida's Sunland Hospital were transferred to the new and improved site in Tallahassee.

Sunland Hospital in Pine Hills became the benefactor and even passed its name to the Tallahassee hospital, which gained much attention from both the media and locals. There have been many unexplained paranormal events in recent times, but Sunland was quite prosperous for many years, and why such a large and powerful state hospital chain would close its doors seemingly overnight would appear to be the real mystery. Was it a lack of money or state funding? Was it the negative press that is rumored to have circulated during that time? Or was this location cursed from the start?

There are a few theories as to why Sunland closed its doors. The first theory is that many of the staff and residents were contracting lung cancer due to the asbestos insulation. This would seem logical, as so many buildings did indeed use this form of insulation in the 1950s. The second theory, as told to me by an ex-employee of Sunland, was that there was an obvious fire hazard in the building, which would have killed the residents on the upper floors if a fire had started. This seems logical too, but why not repair the fire hazard instead of closing the hospital altogether?

The third theory disturbs me the most, and I certainly hope it is untrue, but many of the people I interviewed told of gross mistreatment and medical neglect. Thus, after state inspections found evidence of such horrors, the hospital was forced to close its doors for good. Having worked as a mental health counselor for many years, I can verify that such neglect and mistreatment of patients would certainly warrant closing. In those days, however, experimentation and mistreatment were almost customary and the patients' rights were not as protected as they are today.

The last theory is my favorite and most certainly falls within the realm of ghosts and the supernatural—that the property is itself cursed or haunted. We must remember that Florida was home to many ancient peoples once, inhabited by the Native Americans centuries before Europeans discovered the joys of the Sunshine State. With this in mind, it is easy to see why it might be cursed. With so many years of violence and wars, diseases that literally wiped out entire tribes, and of course, modern construction disturbing sacred burial sites, it stands to reason that the dead might be restless.

From the fateful day it closed in 1983 until the day of its destruction in 2006, Sunland Hospital held an almost surreal quality about it. The tall, barbwire fence draped around the rotting building certainly created a foreboding air, as did the unkept grass and the broken shards of glass that were scattered about, leaving only blank window openings to loom over bystanders. Without a doubt, the whole place just felt wrong, as if the living were just not welcome there.

Ghostly Legends and Haunted Folklore

Although finding the exact history and background of Sunland is close to impossible, the legends and folklore appear to follow a common course that is uniform to practically everyone who explored the hospital's wreckage. Of the people I interviewed, almost everyone seemed to have had similar experiences. The primary feeling was initially excitement. Once inside the huge, lumbering building, however, their feelings soon turned to dread, as if they were being watched. Some actually told me that they heard voices telling them to "Get Out!" or "Go Away!" Those folks had been foolishly compelled to challenge the authorities and go beyond the barbwire fence to explore within the darkened rooms and corriders, risking exposure to asbestos. They claimed to have experienced countless strange and unexplainable things while inside—things that had some people running for safety.

From the outside, in the parking lot, a visitor might have heard sounds of moaning and whimpering, or even an audible scream from a distant part of the hospital. As the witness surveyed the premises, he or she would have eventually found a rusted and decrepit hospital bed on one side of the building. When the old bed was discovered, many would claim that it shivered and shook as soon as they approached it, as if the patient who once occupied it were responding in fear, as perhaps he or she did in life.

In addition to this, there were many reports of cold spots throughout the area, in all seasons. This of course is believed to be evidence of a classic haunting—the cold spot can appear virtually anywhere, and creates a feeling as if a door has suddenly opened or closed. This phenomenon apparently occurred throughout the corridors of the old building, according to one of my informants, who felt the cold spots when walking past the old, totally enclosed steel cages that line some of the halls of the second and third floors. As these cages were used to keep unruly babies and children confined, oftentimes for hours at a time, it would seem logical that such tormenting would have left something behind.

If the presence of cold spots wasn't enough, the occasional scream was certainly more unnerving. In addition to screams heard from both the inside and outside, the sounds of muffled crying were also reported. From time to time people heard the sounds of a dog whimpering as well, its tags or chains jingling as if it were running down the corridors. According to some documents, the hospital once used dogs and other animals in "pet therapy" sessions with the children. This might explain some of these creepy sounds, as the animals would have created a very special bond with the children, thus possibly creating a strong psychical bond as well.

Ghost lights were also sometimes seen streaking through the corridors of Sunland late at night. Naturally, passersby might have thought these lights were nothing more than vagrants, teenagers, or transients running around inside, but when the police investigated, they never found more than the dead and decaying hulk of a once active and bustling hospital.

And then there were the orbs. This phenomenon has in recent years become the quintessential experience in modern ghost hunting, and it has also become the staple of almost all photographic research of ghosts and apparitions. These small, translucent balls of light, or what's believed to be energy from the dead, are have been seen in reputedly haunted locations since the formal use of photography. Though researchers have only recently noticed orbs on much older photographs, the debate as to the authenticity of this phenomena being paranormal remains steadfast in psychical academia. Whether or not this phenomenon is in fact related to paranormal activity is indeed the question. But whatever orbs really are, Sunland had an abundance of them.

As people drove by Sunland at dusk or in the early morning hours, faces of people would sometimes be seen staring out the broken windows, complete with sad demeanors and sullen expressions. These "shadow people" as they have come to be known, were sometimes reported flirting through the hallways and open doors, evaporating before the witness could get a well-focused look. Historically, though at first witnesses who observed such entities might have simply thought they were watching a genuine living person creeping through the corridors, or walking by the windows, they soon learned otherwise when the deceptive shadows vanished right before their eyes.

With all the oral traditions about Sunland and its ghostly reputation, I felt it necessary to give the haunted hospital my full attention. Although Sunland had the added reputation of being off the beaten path, I decided to take the challenge. In the end, the Sunland expedition was well worth the effort.

It was a Saturday morning in October of 2004 when two associates and I arrived at the gates of the old Sunland Hospital. It was a bright morning. There was a gentle breeze and the birds were singing, but the building, that immense decaying structure, seemed strangely alive that day. The feeling that we got was one of sheer amazement, yet we all knew that the dangers here were very real. The dangers of hostile vandals or transients were certainly on our minds, but we also feared the building itself. As the hospital was locked up and abandoned in 1983, it has had a lot of time to decompose and wither away.

The first thing we did was walk around the perimeter of the complex to scope the grounds and get an idea of the layout of the building. Then we started taking photographs at every angle with both digital and 35 mm cameras. The purpose was to create a control group and an experimental database of photos, so we could compare the results of both types of film. We made a video of our actions, as well as an audiotape of what each investigator was doing at that particular time.

The odd sounds began almost immediately. The sounds of things falling, thuds, and glass breaking were apparent to everyone and from time to time a door would slam, echoing throughout the corridors. After a while of this, we decided that the wind may have been responsible and continued our survey.

As we walked completely around the complex, we found a series of intricate sidewalks, half-buried under years of dirt and overgrown grass and weeds. These labyrinths of sidewalks lead out to the wooded area, deep within the forgotten thickets. There we stumbled upon the remains of the old therapeutic wading pool, used for the physically disabled. This pool was completely filled with dirt and covered with a heavy moss, except the gnarled handhold bars, which jutted out of the earth, rusting away. We also found the remains of a playground, which resembled something right out of a ghost town: twisted and rusted, the swings eerily swayed back and forth.

As we found our way out of the thickets, we came upon the rear entrance of the building, apparently used as an ambulance bay. The true threat of the old hospital became clear when we found gaping manholes, half-filled with trash and rancid water collected over the many years. Some of these manholes were clearly fifteen to twenty feet deep. Anyone walking around there at night could easily have become a ghost himself with dangers like that.

As we continued, I found the two side entrances open. One was the doorway to a boiler room, the other an old fire escape door. As we looked in, only darkness peered out, except for the occasional ray of daylight shining through the broken windows down the long corridors. Once inside the main corridor, it was apparent that traveling through the entire building was out of the question, as the ceiling panels hung in tatters, and broken pipes and electrical wires were everywhere. In the corridors, the remains of desks, chairs, and ripped-out doors lay all around, as if a tornado had gone through. And the occasional sound of a door slamming or a pane of glass falling to the ground in the distance was certainly unnerving.

As we approached the elevator, we decided to start taking photographs again. The empty rooms and debris all over the floor only added to our excitement, but when we heard the loud thud down the darkened hallway, the excitement turned to fear. Cautiously, we started to head back down the next section, which appeared to have been a cafeteria, with tin food trays all about and a thick mold growing over the countertops and tables. It looked as if the people who once occupied this place just got up and left. The entire area had an eerie glow because of the way the moldy windows and broken panes let in the daylight. The smell of musty, decaying plaster and stagnant water filled the air.

The hallways seemed to sprawl in all directions, leading to abandoned offices and darkened reception areas; old files and medical records were thrown all about the floor. There was a constant dripping of water, which had been rippling down the now slimy walls from the pooled rain on the roof for at least nineteen years. The whole scene was indescribably creepy. And our hopes for finding a potentially haunted location came with what followed.

As we continued to walk throughout the first floor, taking in all the sights, we started to hear what seemed to be a low muttering coming from the back section of the lower half of the building. Armed only with our flashlights and cameras, we started toward it, only to stop dead in our tracks when we heard movement in an area behind a large half-opened metal door. Our flashlights were strong enough to penetrate the darkness, and I slowly walked in. Not knowing what to expect, I was naturally on alert and ready to run out of there in a second if I saw anything even remotely dangerous. Thankfully, however, there was no one in there, just bare tile walls with stainless steel racks that went to the ceiling, and a few black vinyl bags staked neatly to one end. It did not take me long to realize that I was standing in the hospital's morgue, and with this revelation, I turned and started to walk out. As I did so, leaving the room again in darkness, we once again heard what sounded like muffled mumbling coming from nowhere else but the room I just left.

As we all hurried our pace away from the now darkened morgue, we heard sounds as if someone were walking around within that same room. Now, I know there was no one in that room because I was just there, and the rest of this section of the building was completely barren, outside of the wreckage and debris. At that point, we all decided to end our investigation that day and go home. I can honestly say that the incident had the hairs standing up on my neck and had me looking over my shoulder the whole time I was walking up the ramp and out to the main corridor.

Sunland Hospital—A Final Farewell

In retrospect, Sunland Hospital certainly had an interesting existence, and a history far more secretive than we could ever have guessed. The fact that there were so many strange occurrences only made us wonder: why? Without a doubt, those who dwelled there were full of strong emotions that history shows will sometimes etch themselves to the surroundings. The building may have become a canvas of sorts, painted with these emotions, mostly of rage and sorrow.

Was Sunland Hospital haunted? Most believe it was. Even though the entire building—along with the old therapeutic pool and all the abandoned sidewalks—was torn down in November of 2006, and though the land was churned and new grass put down for possible buyers, the whole place just looks unnatural. If you're in the Tallahassee area, do pay your respects to the site of Florida's hospital of horrors, where unbelievable things took place both during and after its closing more than two decades ago. It would be impossible to say whether or not the land itself will be haunted now that the old hospital is gone and the Sunland legacy has ended. However, one must keep in mind the possibility that the impact left by the unbelievable hardships that occurred there and the lost tormented souls said to reside in the Sunland's once decaying walls and water-filled innards may have been more profound than we might imagine. Try to remember all the lost dreams and shattered hopes that once lived and died at this location. Remember also that within the nearby woods and thorny thickets exists a rather large pauper's graveyard filled with the bodies of forgotten men, women and children, forever to remain in obscurity. Such is all that remains of Sunland Hospital. Therefore, remember the exploits of this once famous and infamous hospital of yesteryear, and reflect on what may become of the new structure that now rests over its old foundation and forgotten cemetery.

Today, a residential complex called the Victoria Grand Apartments rests were the old hospital once stood. The complex's brochure reads "Victoria Grand Apartments...The Difference between Living and Living Grand!," a statement that sets up such an ironic contrast to the many lost and forgotten souls who may have suffered at Sunland Hospital and wandered its halls until the end. And indeed, I can't help wondering if the new residents of these luxury apartments will experience the otherworldly, as so many people did before this new building's foundation was poured into place.

Victoria Grand Apartments is located at 2350 Phillips Road, Tallahassee, Florida. For more information, call (850) 329-6200, or visit their website: www.victoriagrand.com

St. Augustine

11

The City of St. Augustine

America's Oldest and Most Haunted City

A Little History

When we think of ancient cities in the United States, we will most likely think of cities like Boston or Philadelphia as the oldest. In truth, Saint Augustine, located in northeast Florida, was the first city to be settled by Europeans in the Americas. The Spanish explorer Ponce de León was the first known visitor to land on the shores of St. Augustine in 1513, and in 1565 Pedro Menéndez de Avilés founded St. Augustine. Thus, St. Augustine was already close to seventy years old when the Pilgrims landed at Plymouth Rock.

After more than five centuries, enduring periods of Spanish, English, and American rule, sacked by pirates and countless enemies from across the sea, St. Augustine has stood strong through it all. It stands to reason that a city with such a colorful and violent past would be haunted. Indeed, it is so haunted that many researchers of the paranormal have dubbed St. Augustine the most haunted city in America.

Practically everything you see in this wonderful town is historic. St. Augustine, as the oldest continuously occupied European settlement in North America, has a downtown Historic District brimming

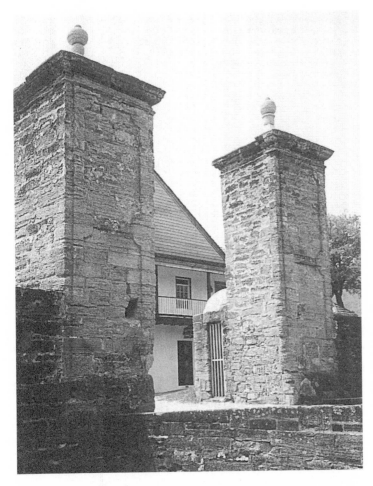

St. Augustine's Main Gates

with antiquities. Horse-drawn carriages march down the ancient streets, lined on either side with houses built over the last two centuries. The air of this city is both modestly modern and downright ancient.

With several excellent bed and breakfasts in town, including the St. Francis Inn and the Casablanca Inn, you can stay in a house that is well over 200 years old, but with the added amenities of any five-star hotel. One of the oldest known homes in St. Augustine is the

Gonzalez Alvarez House, built in 1723. It now serves as a museum devoted to the St. Augustine's domestic and social history, documenting everything from the Spanish Colonial period through the British occupation to the present day. There is also the oldest operating drugstore, which also serves as a museum representing a turn-of-the-century general store and pharmacy. Just up the street is the legendary Fountain of Youth, which continues to sell the same spring water that Ponce de León was believed to drink as the alleged source of everlasting life.

The Huguenot Cemetery, one of St. Augustine's original public burial grounds, was named in honor of the French adventurer-explorers, who came to the area at about the same time as the Spaniards. This cemetery served as the main graveyard for French immigrants and other Protestants for many years and silently sits across from the original 1718 city gates. This humble cemetery was one of the main burial grounds used after one of St. Augustine's worst yellow fever outbreaks in the early part of the nineteenth century. Once inside the city gates, you will find the Spanish Quarter Village, a quaint, educational look into St. Augustine's past. The museum consists of authentic recreations of original buildings and gardens complete with costumed reenactors, who describe daily life in St. Augustine during the mid eighteenth century from both the Spanish and English points of view—for the English ruled from 1763 to 1783.

During your stroll down the cobblestone road in the Spanish Village, you'll come to the Peso de Burgo-Pellicer House, which housed Minorcan plantation workers in the 1770s. There you will see the reenactments of everyday life, such as how the mill would have operated, cooking techniques, and building tools and furniture, as well as a brief demonstration of how those workers pleaded with the governor to be freed from their slavery. All in all, the Spanish Village illustrates the culture and attitudes of seventeenth- and eighteenth-century living.

The Basilica Cathedral of St. Augustine has been in existence since the mid-1600s, but was rebuilt in 1797. The early colonial facade and tower give St. Augustine a look of ancient piety as well as its historic silhouette from land and sea. The Plaza de la Constitution has served as the public marketplace for St. Augustine's residents since the late 1590s. The proud statue of Juan Ponce de León stands at its center, pointing toward the sea as a reminder of Spain's conquest of the seas.

The pride of St. Augustine's military past, the Castillo de San Marcos National Monument, rests seaside as if still waiting to defend its beloved city from intruders. Today, the fort serves as a reminder of Florida's less peaceful times and as a source of education for young and old alike. There are daily tours through the fort, with rangers that will guide you through the cold gunpowder chambers and teach about the fort's unique construction and what life was like for the soldiers who lived there. The cannons are fired periodically as part of reenactments. And throughout the year, there are many special events with costumed reenactors to give the visitor a good look at what ancient times might have looked like.

Because St. Augustine holds so many ghostly legends and tales of hauntings, I have listed a few of the most reputedly haunted locations that may be seen when visiting this glorious city. From the gates to the bridges of the town and all in between, St. Augustine is a city that absolutely must be visited. If you have a love for all things ancient or if you long to hear that perfect ghost story or haunted folk tale, then come to St. Augustine.

Enjoy the glory of this charming walk through history, but during it all, try to remember the violent and horrific wars that took place here, the cutthroat pirates that pillaged the city and its people. Try to remember the lost loves and the broken dreams these violent events may have left behind over the centuries. Try to imagine all the spirits that have walked these streets and have lived in these ancient homes now turned into the charming businesses we see today. Who knows? Perhaps the bed and breakfast you will be staying in is haunted, or perhaps the restaurant you will dine in has a ghost or two. This is St. Augustine after all, the most haunted city in America.

There are numerous mysterious legends of ghosts, haunted places, and other paranormal events, which the residents and visitors of St. Augustine have spoken of over the years. One of the most popular legends of St. Augustine's ghosts involves a young girl standing near the city's main gates. These sturdy gates, which date back to 1739, have seen the march of countless soldiers and sailors.

As the story goes, in 1821 a yellow fever epidemic was besieging the ancient city. One of its victims was a girl named Elisabeth, a young, pretty girl around the age of thirteen. History tells us that she was the last of her family—her father long since dead while at sea, her brother and mother both lost to the epidemic. The sick and confused little Elisabeth, after a few days with no one able to help her, now ravaged by the same sickness, wandered through the streets of St. Augustine. Dazed and confused from fever, she came upon the city gates, where she was said to have once played with her young companions. She held the gates, collapsed, and expired on that spot.

From that night to the present, she has been seen by the main gates, dressed in the tattered white sleeping garments she wore the day she died, playing and dancing just as she had done so many years before. Locals say that little Elisabeth can sometimes be seen in the wee hours of the morning, usually around 2:00 or 3:00 A.M. She can sometimes be heard giggling as she skips and dances around the gates. Although her time of death would have been horrific considering the circumstances, in death she appears to be content and even happy with her haunting ground. Stories like Elisabeth's are not uncommon in the ancient city. Indeed, psychics, parapsychologists, and amateur paranormal investigators have made many claims that virtually every stone in this city, in one form or another, is literally a spirit-conducting generator for the ethereal world. It is believed that every location here has collected and stored many centuries' worth of various psychic energies . . . both the good and the bad.

The ancient American Indians knew the special quality this land held, as many of these Indian chiefs have claimed that the St. Augustine land is sacred, with spirits that roam freely. From every plank of ancient wood to each of the ancient stones used in the streets and the buildings, St. Augustine is a haunted city.

12
Castillo de San Marcos

An Eerie Glow and the Scent of Orange Blossoms

A Little History

The Castillo de San Marcos is St. Augustine's National Monument by the waters of Matanzas Bay. This star-shaped fortress has guarded the city for more than 300 years. When it was finally completed in 1672, a seventeenth-century masterpiece of construction, it was so expensive to build that the king of Spain said the walls must have been made with silver. In truth, however, the walls were made of crushed seashells and limestone, a material known as coquina.

The Castillo de San Marcos is an excellent design, especially for sea-to-land combat. The Spanish engineers utilized a square pattern and added diamond-shaped fortified walls called "bastions" at each corner of the structure, which made its attackers vulnerable to crossfire. When the visitors go back to their bed and breakfasts, and when rangers go home for the night, the fort on the Matanzas Bay seems to come alive again.

It was the summer of 1784, shortly after England had ceded Florida's northern lands back to Spain, that the Spanish set up shop in the ancient city once again. The fort was in partial command by a

Colonel Martí, a stern and jealous middle-aged man with a long and illustrious military history. Dolores was his young and quite beautiful wife, who always commanded the attention of all the soldiers. When Colonel Martí and Dolores arrived from Spain that summer, everything had changed for them. History and legend tell us that Colonel Martí hated his new assignment with a passion, as he considered it unworthy of a man with such an excellent military background. St. Augustine was just too isolated a military post, meant more for the soldier who wanted to wind down after a long military career or for a soldier who deserved punishment. For one thing, the fort was too heavily dependent on outside sources for its supplies, and it has been said that the bitter colonel felt that the city wasn't worth defending at all.

The beautiful Dolores was much younger than the colonel and was equally unhappy with the move, not to mention the fact that she had fallen out of love with her overbearing husband, making the matter all the more painful. With the constant biting of mosquitoes, yellow fever, and the intimidating Indians roaming the woodlands and marshes near the fort, the Castillo de San Marcos was quickly becoming her prison—one of the few feelings that the colonel and Dolores had in common.

During the weeks that followed, Dolores caught the eye of one particular officer at the fort, a Captain Manuel Abela. The captain had all the right qualities of a dashing and adventurous military officer, and for Dolores, the pleasant, confidant, and handsome young officer was a pleasant change from her now old and miserable husband. It wasn't long before the two began to exchange glances and kind words and then, one thing led to another and they fell in love. They would meet when the colonel was with his advisors, or when he was away from the fort. During the winter and spring months, there were many rendezvous, during the mornings or during afternoon siesta when the streets were empty, in the shadows of an empty alley or in the orange groves near the river. Their love was as strong as the might of the military her husband served, but this would not last forever . . . or would it?

One day, Colonel Martí summoned Captain Abela for a military conference to go over the maps of the surrounding waters. When Colonel Martí sent for the captain, the dashing officer was in the colonel's personal quarters with the lovely Dolores. The captain had the faith of his men, and they all looked away from the adulterous affair and spoke nothing of it, but the captain's luck was soon to run out.

As this kind of military conference was routine in the fort, the captain acted cool and unworried about meeting his lover's husband, his colonel and commander. When the meeting was over, and the young captain walked past the colonel, a strange feeling came over Colonel Martí, as he was distracted by something he could not explain. For a moment, he was sure he detected a scent of sweet orange blossoms. . . .

The affair was a hot and passionate one, and after a while, both Dolores and the dashing captain let their guards down, becoming cavalier in their attitudes and showing displays of passion in plain day. And it didn't take long for the colonel to hear the rumors of the affair. Colonel Martí decided to wait in the shadows of the orchard and in old alleyways to see if these terrible rumors were true. And, sure enough, when the rest of the town was enjoying the siesta, the captain and Dolores were seen together in a lover's embrace. When Colonel Martí's worst nightmare finally was confirmed, his rage began to boil. He was devising a plan of revenge, and because this act of adultery was embarrassing and degrading to Colonel Martí's reputation, his plan had to be carried out in secret.

While Captain Abela and Dolores were making love a few days later, the colonel was making plans to exact the proper revenge for the dishonest act. Colonel Martí had a few soldiers dig away at some of the stone walls of the gunpowder chambers in the lower levels of the fort. These dark and damp sections of the fort were perfect for what he had planned. Because this area of the fort could not have an open flame in it, due to the volatile gunpowder that was stored there, it was almost always blanketed in darkness . . . perfect for hiding something. It wasn't long until a small chamber around five feet by six feet was showing neatly and four iron fish-eye screws were placed deep in the wall within. There was a stack of stone bricks by the entrance of this chamber, a bucket of fresh mortar, and a spade. This was the place where the colonel would have his satisfaction. The following day, a rainy day, the colonel and Dolores were walking through the fort. It was at this time that the captain was given a message to go to the gunpowder chambers for an inspection. Seeing an opportunity for a secret tryst, he took Dolores along.

With only the light of a lantern hanging from the outside hallway, the colonel drew his gun on the two lovers. With a look of shock, the captain and Dolores asked why he would do such a thing, but Colonel Martí only stood there with a look of utter rage on his face. After a moment, the colonel demanded that Dolores lock the shackles hanging from the wall onto Captain Abela's wrist. When this was done, Colonel Martí took Dolores by the throat and slammed her against the wall of the chamber. Wrestling to lock the other set of shackles unto her wrists, he would hear nothing of her cries and pleas. The colonel stood back to watch with a demonic hatred the two people who had shamed him, but his work was not done yet.

The colonel silently went about placing the bricks on top of each other, mortar in between, forming a nice, sturdy wall. Although Captain Abela's screams and Dolores's crying were loud and echoed throughout the chambers, their pleas for forgiveness went unheard, because that morning Colonel Martí had taken precautions. He had ordered the soldiers to stand guard around the outer perimeter to keep lookout for any approaching ships, even though the soldiers knew there would be no ships coming. The command was followed and the wall was finished . . . the deed was done.

Captain Abela was reported missing a few days later, but what of Dolores? Where did the colonel's lovely wife go? Colonel Martí had announced that Captain Abela was sent to Cuba on a secret mission and that Dolores had become seriously ill and had to be sent to recuperate in Mexico with family until she could return to Spain to stay at his estate.

The colonel's plan had worked flawlessly and his revenge was secure. Neither Captain Abela nor Dolores Martí were ever seen again. The rule of Spain came and went, and people finally forgot about the beautiful Dolores and the dashing captain. Yet, almost from the time of their disappearance, many soldiers spoke of hearing the dull sounds of crying and moans echoing through the chamber walkways, accompanied by the subtle scent of orange blossoms. Nobody was certain where this scent could possibly come from, especially within the bowels of the empty fort during the wee hours of the morning, but there were a few soldiers who knew that scent and would instantly remember Dolores Martí.

Ghostly Legends and Haunted Folklore

For almost two centuries the sounds of moans and as well as the drifting scent of orange blossoms and sometimes roses would be in the air late at night. From soldiers to visitors, people have spoken of the strange events that would sometimes take place in and around the fort.

On July 21, 1833, while testing the cannons for accuracy, the vibrations from the newer, more powerful cannons cracked the flooring on which they sat, breaking through and smashing down to the empty chambers below. As some of the men were investigating the damage below, a Lieutenant Stephan Tuttle with the United States Army Corps of Engineers found the crushed room with the cannon sticking out and a section of wall behind it, where no such wall should have been. When he investigated further, he noticed that it sounded hollow when he tapped it. Using the tip from his bayonet, Lt. Tuttle chipped the mortar away, and it wasn't long until he was able to remove some of the stones from the strange wall. When he did this, a gust of perfumed air like the scent of sweet oranges blew past him. Holding his lantern high, he peered in, only to step back in astonishment. The illumination from the lantern lit up the yellowish-white glow of two skeletons chained to a wall, embracing each other. Dolores Martí and Captain Manuel Abela were finally found. Had Colonel Martí chained them to the wall of the dungeon-like gunpowder chamber then sealed them alive behind a thick wall of coquina?

The soldier who opened the ghastly tomb later told of a sweet, subtle fragrance that filled the underground passageway when he removed

The lower level of the Castillo de San Marcos

the blocks, a scent that remained the entire time he was in the chamber, but vanished when he returned with others moments later. Did the exploring engineer release the tormented spirits of these two murdered lovers? Perhaps, but from time to time the scent of sweet orange blossoms can still be detected in and around the great fort.

People who visit the ancient fortress today say there is a strange glow emanating in the shadowy darkness at the spot where the lovers were murdered. And when that glow is seen, a sweet fragrance, like the scent of a lady's fine perfume, floats on the cool, dank air.

Because the story may have been told and retold over the years, there is of course the possibility that much of the truth has been altered, but the legend has existed at least since the late eighteenth century. People visiting the fort, some of the park rangers, and even some of the reenactors have witnessed many strange things taking place during the wee hours of the morning.

A dark-haired young woman wearing a white flowing dress is sometimes seen walking the grounds of the fort, appearing sad and melancholy, then simply vanishing behind the walls. Another ghost seen here is said to be a young Spanish soldier searching for something on the grounds by the fort's main gates. Legend tells us that this soldier was searching for a ring that was given to him by his beloved wife-to-be back in Spain. While in the heat of his search, an enemy ship fired its cannons at the fort and killed this soldier instantly.

The ghost of another young soldier is sometimes seen after sundown leaning up against the outside wall facing the bay. He seems so real and lifelike that visitors have approached to asked questions about his costume, only to watch him dissolve before their eyes. Some of the other unusual occurrences include what sounds like the echoes of a battle when you place your ears to the fort's walls. It is said you can hear cannon fire and the soldiers screaming commands to the ghostly men of the fort.

At night and during the early hours of morning, witnesses have claimed to see the movement of people walking the battlement, as if soldiers on duty. Although only silhouettes of people, they have been so realistic that the St. Augustine police have searched for trespassers on more than one occasion. When they look around, they only find an empty fort.

Afterthoughts

The Castillo de San Marcos has an interesting haunted history and certainly the legend of the cruel Colonel Martí, his wayward wife Dolores, and her soldier lover is a tragic love story. Although the story ends somewhat unhappily, it's rewarding to know that love can outlast the grave.

The ghosts and specters that wander the grounds casting an eerie glow or giving off a lovely scent tell us that history lives on. As the

Castillo de San Marcos is the oldest fort in the United States, it's not hard to imagine all the pain and hardships it has seen. From British warships to the galleons of the Spanish armada and even the plundering of pirates, the fort stood strong. When visiting St. Augustine's grand fort, enjoy the history it offers, walk down the corridors and on the battlement. Listen to the reenactor scream out his commands and hear the cannon's roar, but keep an eye out for a spirit or two. See if you too can catch a scent of lovely Dolores's orange blossom perfume.

13

The Old Spanish Hospital

Old Soldiers Never Die

A Little History

The Spanish Hospital, located between Artillery and Aviles Streets, is St. Augustine's oldest hospital. Operating from 1784 until 1821, the year Florida became a United States territory, the Spanish Hospital saw its share of grisly events and horrors on a daily basis. There are countless documented names of soldiers that were treated in the hospital, many of whom died there. Now an educational museum, the hospital offers a quaint look into the history of colonial medicine and the realities of war and illness in Florida's colonial past.

The main section of the hospital consists of a medium-sized room with a hearth, a fireplace, and several beds made up for incoming wounded. There's a surgeon's desk, complete with colonial medical instruments—scalpels, bone saws, bullet retractors, mortar and pestles, lancets and blood-letting bowls—as well as an assortment of medicinal herbs hanging from the rafters.

To the rear of the building is the apothecary room, where ancient technicians once mixed the herbs into powders, salves, and ointments from the herb garden behind the building. Several of the actual beds

remain here, as well as pots, chandeliers, and other miscellaneous items from a different time. This back section is a dark and foreboding collection of rooms where one can actually feel the unfortunate past in the sparse, dank quarters where so many died. Needless to say, if there are any ghosts in St. Augustine, you can bet there are a few here. And more than one employee will agree to this.

If working in an eerie location like the old Spanish Hospital, knowing that hundreds of people have died there over the years, isn't enough to spook an employee once in a while, then nothing will. If one is also told that the street in front of the old hospital was once used as a cemetery for the discarded dead and countless amputations, one might have second thoughts about working there altogether.

During the early 1970s the underground water table shifted, causing underground pipes to crack and burst, thus caving in a huge section of the cobblestone street. Because it would have been almost impossible to replace the road completely in a short amount of time, the city decided to remove a section of the street and fix the old broken pipes, then move on to another section, and so on until the task was complete. When they removed the section of road in front of the old hospital, they found the problem pipes and something else—hundreds of human skeletons. A grisly find, but this is St. Augustine after all, a city once devoted to war and tragedy.

The bones consisted of complete skeletons, partial skeletons, arms, hands, legs, feet, and skulls. Apparently, after the surgeons performed an amputation, the technician placed the remains in a long narrow ditch near the curb, then covered it up with dirt. Archaeologists surmised that this must have been a common practice—planting human remains like a farmer would have planted seeds in a field.

The city ultimately decided that because the makeshift cemetery was indeed an ancient site, it should be left alone. So, the bones were returned to the shallow grave, covered with dirt and the bricks neatly replaced—so nice in fact that no tourist would ever suspect that they were walking on a mass grave. Although from the outside the old Spanish Hospital looks rather small and simple, there are those who know the darker side of this museum . . . the restless ghosts!

Ghostly Legends and Haunted Folklore

I had the opportunity to speak with several of the museum's staff, and they were more than open about the many events that took place there over the years. Shannon Pimplelbeck, one of the historical reenactors at the Spanish Hospital, told of several spectral events that had a few employees running out of the hospital for dear life. Shannon tells of one late afternoon, a particularly dark and drizzly day, when one of the female actors was all alone in the hospital. There were no customers at the time, and because of the heavily overcast day, the whole hospital was dark inside, except for the faint candlelight.

As she was finishing up her paperwork for the day, the rain beginning to pelt against the windows and a chill falling over the whole room, she noticed a slight movement at the rear door of the main hospital chamber. As she squinted to look at the doorknob leading into the apothecary, the noise got louder, as if someone were trying to get through. Although this room was now being used as an office for the museum's manager, the lone worker knew full well that the building was empty. The lone employee, now becoming genuinely frightened, picked up her radio and asked if someone would please come back to the hospital because there were strange noises coming from the back rooms. Shannon responded over the now crackling radio to say she was heading back that way and not to worry. It wasn't too long after the radio call that the now thoroughly scared employee saw Shannon and a male employee walking toward her. Just as the recognition of her friends forced her to exclaim, "Thank God," the subtle rapping behind the rear door had become a loud series of thuds. This employee jumped over the counter and ran out into the street past her friends. After finally calming the girl down, the male employee walked through the entire hospital while the two girls waited outside. He found nothing to explain the strange sounds.

Although this particular employee no longer works there, many others have experienced similar phenomena. On several occasions, two or three self-proclaimed psychics have made interesting remarks as to who the spirits are, and although these psychics had visited the Spanish Hospital on separate occasions, there were many similarities in their stories.

Evidently, there is a spirit of an officer who is believed to have died from his wounds during the Seminole Indian Wars in the early part of the nineteenth century. He tried to hold on to life in order to see his wife and child before he died, but he lost too much blood. Although the spirit is said to realize that he is dead, he has decided to stay here for unknown reasons. Some believe that he may be protecting the living from the not-so-friendly spirits that also remain in the hospital. One psychic claimed that this officer soldier could sometimes be seen by the fireplace where his bed once sat. This place, according to the psychic, was so important to the solider in his final days, he goes there and continues to reminisce of his corporeal life. Apparently, as he was dying, he would stare into the fire a think of his family, finally expiring while thinking of his memories. Although he oftentimes appears to be an unhappy spirit, he has been known to assist the living, especially female employees, by protecting them from an angry spirit who seems to take pride in frightening the living.

This other spirit is believed to be that of a woman dressed in black clothing matching a period around the middle part of the nineteenth century. She is said to have been denied entrance into the hospital ward where her husband was dying. Grief stricken and angry, being removed from the hospital by force, the woman slashed her wrists in protest.

Perhaps she thought they would put her in the hospital next to husband. But this was not to be. As the hospital was for military men only, she was left to perish from her injuries. She is said to be an angry spirit now, hateful of the living, especially women. The psychics who have seen her say that she wears black, most likely a result of her committing suicide. She is also believed to be just as jealous in death as she was in life. Moreover, she is responsible for the knocks at the doors and walls and has been known to push people and even pull women's hair. Although the psychics feel that this entity is somewhat nasty, she should not be considered evil, just very angry.

Many of these psychics believe that because the female nurses had prevented the woman in black from visiting her husband before he died, she now harbors a grudge and contempt for all women, resulting in the strange actions toward many of the Spanish Hospital's female employees. So, when visiting the old Spanish Hospital, try to remember the hundreds of men who lay in those beds, alone, sad, and dying. When walking through this dark, antiquated building, especially if you're a woman, also remember to watch your back and beware.

Afterthoughts

There may be more restless souls wandering the streets of St. Augustine, through the many ancient buildings and perhaps even visiting the place where they had died, and the old Spanish Hospital is certainly no exception. The flickering candles, the thuds at the door, and even reports of physical contact should unquestionably give reason to suspect a spirit. As this hospital represents a place where so many had died in such lonely agony, it stands to reason this location would contain a ghost or at least the residue of the tormented souls who suffered here. The gentleman officer who attends to the needs of the museum's female employees or the angry woman in black who stomps and pounds around the hospital seem to simply reflect the tenacity of the human spirit, whether it be one of honor or rage.

When visiting St. Augustine, make sure a visit to the Spanish Hospital is on the list of things to do. Enjoy this brief walk through time, but remember the reality of the hospital and its horror-filled past. Stay on the lookout for strange things that may be lurking in the dark and be sure to listen for a slight rapping on the doors and wall.

14

Flagler College

The Lady in Blue

A Little History

In 1882, Henry Flagler, New York entrepreneur and cofounder of Standard Oil, became interested in St. Augustine for its potential as a winter resort. Flagler's Midas touch stimulated the development of transportation and resorts throughout Florida's east coast. And the Hotel Ponce de Leon was one of the main focal points for it all. Flagler began plans for his "Hotel Ponce" in 1887 by hiring two young, prominent architects from New York City.

The Ponce's Spanish Revival design was so popular that it influenced most of the architecture for southern Florida for the next fifty years. The success of the Ponce de Leon was short lived, however, because in 1895, almost immediately after the grand unveiling, a yellow fever epidemic broke out, and Florida experienced one of the worst freezes in its history. The town never became the winter resort Flagler had hoped, yet many tourists did flock to the area in the early twentieth century, and the Hotel Ponce de Leon was just one of three Flagler Hotels to survive the Great Depression. In the 1940s, however, tourism began to wane, and by the late 1960s, the hotel was forced

to close and become a shadow of Flagler's dreams and of Florida's past. Thankfully, the ornate retired building would eventually become Flagler College, thus writing a new chapter in Florida history.

Flagler College is nestled on nineteen acres of prime land in the heart of the old city. The grand Hotel Ponce de Leon now serves as a centerpiece for the beautiful campus and is listed on the National Register of Historic Places, recognized as Henry Flagler's gift to the city of Saint Augustine. Since 1968, the college has spent millions restoring the historic hotel and building the rest of its campus.

Ghostly Legends and Haunted Folklore

Over the years Flagler College has attracted many ghost stories, most of which take place in the main rotunda of Ponce Hall, now a dormitory. There are also a lot of stories about the fourth floor, which is boarded up and strictly off limits . . . but why?

History tells us that Henry Flagler had little luck with both his wives and his mistresses. One story has it that one mistress in particular, who was angry and jealous of her lover's lack of commitment, hanged herself by a chandelier in one of the fourth floor suites. Being one of the more popular ghost stories at Flagler College, it has been told from student to student since the 1960s. According to many of these students, the room is still completely boarded up, yet some are brave enough to peek through the keyhole to see if they can view the legs and feet of Flagler's mistress still swaying from side to side.

Another time-honored legend concerns the funeral of Henry Flagler, which was held in the main entrance of the hotel. Flagler had insisted that all the doors and windows be opened after his death so that his spirit could be free and not trapped in the hotel forever. His wishes were obeyed, and all the windows and doors were opened just as Flagler had asked. Unfortunately, as a janitor was arriving to work for the day, he noticed the funeral procession. As he was passing the ceremony, he noticed that the main doors and all of the windows were open. He closed them, muttering about a lack of respect for the dead. As soon as he did so, it is said that there was a huge gust of wind that blew from one end of the hall to the other.

One lady attending the funeral, a self-proclaimed psychic, claimed that it was Flagler's spirit trying to get out, but it failed to escape in time. It is believed that his spirit slammed against one of the windows and bounced backward, landing in one of the tiny, quarter-sized tiles of the rotunda, caught there forever. To this very day, just to the left of the main doors at the front of the large rotunda, you can see the face of Henry Flagler, eerily staring at you as if in great thought.

The tile with Henry Flagler's face is interesting enough to say the least, but there are some that believe that the great oil tycoon, Florida's famous hotel and train baron, still walks the stately halls of his beloved Ponce, most likely amused by the fast-paced kids of this college bearing his name.

In the 1970s, a student rooming in Ponce Hall found the tile as he was going to the cafeteria for breakfast. In a light-hearted tradition, as he passed the tile each day he would ask Mr. Flagler to visit him sometime. And, on one early morning, around 6:30 A.M., Henry Flagler did just that. As the story is told, when the young man was waking up that fall morning, dreading having to get up and go to class, he felt a presence standing over him. At first, he thought it was his roommate getting dressed for school, and ignored it for a while, until he remembered his roommate was at home all that week. He opened his eyes suddenly to see who it could be, and to his amazement, the grayish, stern-looking figure of Henry Flagler was staring down on him from the foot of his bed!

As he rubbed his eyes to confirm the event, the figure was gone. Needless to say, this young man did not make idle invitations to ghosts again. Many psychics over the years have claimed to feel the presence of Henry Flagler throughout the entire campus, and even as far south as West Palm Beach in his beloved Whitehall Mansion.

Another popular specter is believed to be that of Mrs. Ida Alice Flagler, Henry's second wife. Ida Alice had many issues in life, primarily issues with mental illness, and in those days they didn't have the advanced mental health therapies like there are today. As Ida's problems grew, Henry was eventually advised by his personal physician to have her put away for a "rest," committing her to a sanitarium. There, she would rant at the walls and finally died of consumption. It would seem, however, that Ida Alice was not ready to leave this earthly plane just yet.

Today, many people—students, professors, and visitors alike—have seen the image of what many feel is Miss Ida Alice. She is said to be much calmer now, walking in the gardens and sometimes on the rotunda looking at the beautifully painted ceilings, which she had always admired in life. Many suspect that Ida Alice was aware of her husband's many affairs, and they had silently torn at her through the years, eventually driving her to madness. Yet, some still believe her sickness was hereditary and her insanity was just a matter of time.

Although Ida Alice's spirit is said to be calm now, she is sometimes seen staring at a section of a plain wood-panel wall in the inner circumference of the great rotunda. Though there is nothing on that wall today, a long-time resident of St. Augustine said that there was once a huge oil painting of Henry Flagler hanging there. Ida Alice is said to stare at the wall for a few minutes and then simply fade away, and so some suggest she still contemplates her life's misery.

We must not forget the spirit that haunts the fourth-floor room of this college, the spirit said to be one of Henry Flagler's mistresses. As Henry was always engaged in one liaison or another, it was only a matter of time before there would be a mishap.

One day, when Ida Alice was making a surprise visit to the Hotel Ponce de Leon, Henry received his usual warning signal from one of his loyal bellboys. Quickly, he had his mistress go to the fourth floor suite to make sure that the women would not meet. The mistress, having this done on so many occasions and feeling rejected and angry because of it, began using drugs as an escape from her pain, and most likely, to get Henry's attention. However, her plan failed, and she became hopelessly addicted to heroin, eventually going insane from the poisoning.

The mistress's usual fourth-floor suite, called "the mirrored suite," was in fact a psychomantium, a room used for altering one's state of

The closed section of Flagler College

mind as well as contacting the dead. Although this room is quite beau-tifully decorated, almost completely covered with mirrors from wall to ceiling, it proved to be too much for the girl, causing her finally to snap. She hanged herself from an ornate chandelier. That night, when Henry sneaked in for a midnight meeting, he found the cold corpse of his concubine.

Today, the room is locked and visitors and students are restricted from the fourth floor, but many of the students still go up there in hopes of catching a glimpse of the swaying mistress. Former students who at one time were allowed to stay in the fourth-floor rooms would swear that that the suicide room would always have weird things happening there. Photographs and posters would never stay on the walls for long, books, radios and other objects would fly off shelves and desks, and many of the kids would awaken to the sounds of screams. Sometimes, those who stayed in that room would claim to see the image of a person hanging from the chandelier, swaying from side to side.

Today the fourth floor is off limits, but from the rear of the building, some claim to see things being thrown around inside, as well as strange lights fluttering around late at night. Although no one has seen this unfortunate spirit clamoring around the hallways of the campus, many believe she is extremely active in her own suite. Perhaps this is the true reason the fourth floor is boarded up and off limits today, perhaps the forgotten mistress is just too angry to live with.

Another famous ghost of Flagler College is known as the "lady in blue." She is by far is the most witnessed ghost in the college. She is believed to have been a guest at the Ponce de Leon Hotel. Oral tradition tells us that while staying there, she was having an affair with a married man, and eventually got pregnant. She had hoped that this man would get a divorce and marry her as he had promised, but he lied, and the lady in blue apparently went mad with anger and sadness. As she ran up to her suite to cry and pack her suitcases, she tripped on her long sky-blue skirt and fell backwards, tumbling down the stairs and breaking her neck. She died in a torrent of tears.

To this day, people have reported seeing her ghost walking slowly through the lobby at night and in the dining room looking for her favorite table, but she only finds unfamiliar furniture, then bows her head and covers her face with her hands. Students have seen the lady in blue crying as she walks through the hallways at night, forever sad at the loss of her love and the baby she never knew.

Without a doubt Flagler College's most heartbreaking ghost, she continues her nocturnal activities to this day. No one is quite sure if she's buried here in one of St. Augustine's graveyards, as locating the hotel's documents is all but impossible today. Some have suggested that her death would have been a threat to the married man she was seeing, and she was buried in secret to stop any possibility of her family bringing legal action against him. Some have suggested that he was from a powerful family that made millions from political endeavors, but no one is quite sure. The one thing that many of the students of Flagler College are sure of is that this sad specter still mourns her loss.

And yes, there's still one more ghost within this paranormally active college. The spirit known is as the lost little boy, and although fairly well known, he seems to be the most difficult to understand. Indeed, there are many conflicting stories about this young specter. Many feel that this child fell from a balcony over the rotunda, others believe he fell down a flight of stairs. Although the story is not quite clear, many students have felt the sensation of someone tapping their shoulder or tugging on their shirts. Some claimed to have heard the voice of a little boy asking them to come outside and play, even though no one claimed to have seen the ghostly child. On occasion, while walking down the hallways late at night, some may hear a child's request for a playmate and then witness a small green ball bouncing down the hallway and into a darkened corner. Confused and a little frightened, those who witnessed the odd event would walk over to the where the ball had rolled to pick it up, only to find nothing and no sign of a child.

The little boy is a paranormal enigma. Although he represents the classic haunting, he seems to portray a spirit with a purpose, most likely an innocent one, or perhaps he is just replaying his youthful behavior. Many have researched the possible identity this spirit, because the death of such a small child would most assuredly be recorded. Apparently, there was indeed a child reported to have died by falling out of a window around the turn of the century, when the college was a bustling hotel.

Another theory, although not admitted by any official of the college, is that in the late 1960s or early 1970s, a teenage boy was visiting his girlfriend in one of the dorms, but this teenager was also watching over his little brother that evening. The older boy, not wanting his younger brother to get in the way of his romantic intentions, told the little brother to stay outside and play. The young boy did just that. He played with his ball, throwing it against the wall and catching it, and then he began climbing on the railings of the balcony.

This legend continues with the boy falling from either the balcony or while sliding down the stair railing, landing on his head and dying instantly. His identity is kept secure for unknown reasons, although his demeanor is relatively benign and somewhat playful. Needless to say, those who witness this event claim to feel a chill in the air and an intense feeling of sadness.

Afterthoughts

Flagler College is truly a haunted realm all its own in America's most haunted city. In addition, although it is a center for wisdom and scholarly thought today, the former Hotel Ponce de Leon certainly had its share of intrigue and hardship. The lady in blue, the angry mistress on the fourth floor, and Miss Ida Alice are all examples of St. Augustine's tormented spirits of her past. The little boy, who is not as active as the other spirits, remains among the college's relatively recent mysteries.

In retrospect, Flagler College is one of those landmarks that will always hold its past, whether good or bad, and the very walls of the ornate building secrete a paranormal residue that cannot go unnoticed. Many visiting psychical researchers feel that this location is truly unique. Perhaps the ghosts here are simple replays of the landmark's historical past, or perhaps these spirits remain enthralled with their surroundings. The answer will not come until it is our time to learn for ourselves.

15

Casa Monica Hotel

Strange Whispers

A Little History

The Casa Monica, once known as the Cordova Hotel, was designed, and constructed in 1887 by New England architect Franklin W. Smith. It opened its doors on January 1, 1888. By April of that same year, because of management and financial problems, Henry Flagler would purchase the Casa Monica Hotel from Franklin Smith, complete with all its furnishings, for $325,000.

Renamed the Cordova, the hotel thrived under Flagler and became known for its lavish parties, masquerades, and charity balls. In 1903, the Cordova Hotel and the nearby Alcazar Hotel merged to become the Alcazar Annex. Once again, after enduring many financial hardships, primarily the Great Depression, the hotel would close its doors in the spring of 1932.

The once stately Cordova Hotel would sit as a looming hulk, deserted and almost forgotten. By the early 1960s, the old Cordova Hotel was purchased by the St. Johns County Commission to be used as a courthouse, and the St. Johns County Courthouse opened its doors in 1964.

In 1997, an Orlando architectural firm purchased the courthouse in order to return the building's original charm by recreating the luxurious hotel. In 1999, the Casa Monica Hotel was again opened to the public. The spirit of the old Cordova Hotel was reborn with all the stately charm it once had. Indeed, even Spain's King Juan Carlos I and Queen Sophia enjoyed a visit, as well as many political figures and Hollywood stars, all ushering in a new era for the Casa Monica Hotel.

The 138-room, castle-like hotel is an enchanting blend of Spanish and Moorish architecture, with many intricate balconies all around it. There is an arched carriage entrance, thousands of hand-painted tiles from Italy, and five majestic tower suites. Inside, the Moorish-style columns and the many pieces of artwork create a perfect environment for socializing, listening to the piano while enjoying a cocktail in the nearby lounge, or just relaxing after a long day of shopping and sightseeing in historic St. Augustine.

Ghostly Legends and Haunted Folklore

Unlike many other hotels and inns throughout St. Augustine that enjoy telling visitors about their resident ghosts, the Casa Monica Hotel will not openly share such stories with their guests. Apparently, the Casa Monica Hotel chooses to serve its guests in a refined manner instead of embellishing its ghostly lore. And of course, when it literally serves kings and queens, the last thing they should know is that there are a few ghosts in their hotel. Fortunately, however, there are a few employees that will share a story or two.

I can recall hearing several stories about the Casa Monica Hotel while visiting St. Augustine a few years ago. I spoke one afternoon with a bellhop, a young student from the nearby Flagler College who worked at the Casa Monica part time. He told me that the primary paranormal events to take place in the hotel are mostly strange noises, like someone whispering. These whispers are as though someone is talking from off in the distance or during a windstorm, and the words cannot be deciphered. Moreover, guests will sometimes call down to the front desk to report such sounds coming from the hallways. The hallways will always be found empty, and the whispering sounds that were there a moment ago will simply cease when guests open their doors to see who might be there. This is strange, but there is something else in the Casa Monica Hotel.

This bellhop continued to tell me of another odd occurrence, though rare. Apparently, the apparition of a nicely dressed gentleman, wearing a gray-and-black-striped suit and hat resembling the style of the late 1920s, is seen walking in the corridors late in the evenings. Although nobody seems to know who this spirit might have been in life, many think he committed suicide.

Although there are no records of, or at least no records shared about a suicide in the early days of the Cordova Hotel, after the stock market crash of 1929 there were many resulting suicides. This spirit may have been among those.

This specter has even been reported to enter the rooms of several guests over the years. The bellhop continued to tell me of one such incident that took place one fall evening in 2000. Evidently, a visiting couple called the front desk complaining that a man had just walked into their room, gone into their bathroom, and then vanished. Understandably frightened, the husband had walked in the bathroom after the intruder but found it empty, no trace of a man ever being there. After the staff looked through the guest's room and throughout the entire hotel for a man matching that description, they found no one.

On another occasion in that same year, another couple reported an almost identical incident. This time, however, the couple woke up to see a figure standing over the front table in their room, near the television. They said it was a man who was turned away from them and looking down at something. When the husband began to sit up in his bed to get a look at this intruder, he made enough noise to alert the shadowy man, who then walked straight through the door of the room and into the hallway. When the couple tuned on the bedside light and got up to open their door, they noticed heavy footprints in the hotel's thick carpet. The footprints led nowhere.

Although this phantom intruder has been silent in the last year, footprints will every now and again be seen in the rooms of unnerved guests. This entity has never harmed anyone; thankfully, his only crime seems to be curiosity.

Afterthoughts

Although the Casa Monica Hotel chooses to remain off St. Augustine's many guided ghost tours, the visitors taking one of those ghost tours will no doubt hear of the hotel's phantom who enjoys looking in on the Casa Monica's guests. Indeed, even if you're not staying in this gorgeous hotel, you may walk through its beautiful lobby or have a drink in the adjacent lounge. Perhaps you will be lucky enough to find someone to tell you a story or two about the Casa Monica ghost. Maybe you will hear the faint whispering from someone you will never see. . . .

When visiting the Casa Monica Hotel, enjoy the many amenities it has to offer, but try to remember the many people who have walked through those corridors over the last one hundred years. Remember that St. Augustine is, after all, the most haunted city in the United States, and what ghost wouldn't want to stay there?

The Casa Monica Hotel is located at 95 Cordova Street, St. Augustine, Florida. You may call for reservations and information at 904-827-1888 or 800-648-1888.

16

St. Francis Inn

Miss Lily and her Soldier Lover

A Little History

The St. Francis Inn is one of St. Augustine's oldest bed and breakfasts, dating back to 1791. Just around the corner from the oldest house in St. Augustine, it represents a rich history in America's oldest city, brimming with stories of love and love lost, of life and death. The rich history and culture found its beginning during the city's Second Spanish Colonial Period. The architecture reflects a time when safety and protection against invaders was paramount. This was an understandable concern, as the threat of invasion was so strong that houses had to be constructed to serve as fortresses against those who would attempt to occupy their town.

Although the records of St. Augustine's early years are not entirely complete, we know that Gaspar Garcia, a sergeant in the Cuban army, was the St. Francis's first official owner. Garcia was granted this section of land by the king of Spain himself. In 1802, the property was bought by a ship's captain named Juan Ruggiers, whose family estate held the land until the early years of American rule in Florida.

Many subsequent owners and residents included other military figures, such as Colonel Thomas Henry Dummett, a retired officer with Britain's Royal Marines, who bought the house in 1838. Dummett's daughter eventually turned the building into an inn in 1845. Several families owned the St. Francis Inn over the many years, mostly military families, and although all the records of the inn's past have been lost, we know that it has changed very little.

At one point there was a maidservant named Lily who worked for a prominent military family that owned the inn. She is believed to have been a slave woman from Barbados, and is said to have been one of the most beautiful women in St. Augustine during that time. It was only a matter of time before a young Spanish soldier fell in love with her. The two of them held their love affair secret for some time, sneaking into the rooms of the inn to make love. One day the owner of the home, a military officer, walked in on the two lovers, and screamed at them in rage. Their love was not to take place under his roof, or anywhere else for that matter. It was a direct order.

The soldier, denied love with Lily, could not live without her, and decided to climb the stairs to a third-floor room for one final mission. Overlooking the quaint courtyard below where the two would go to embrace, he now only saw what he could no longer have. No one saw the rope under his arm as he was climbing the stairs. The soldier is said to have stood on a chair, anchored the rope to a rafter, placed the noose around his neck, and leapt. His escape from a tormenting pain that would not heal was completed, but his story does not end here.

Ghostly Legends and Haunted Folklore

Over the years, the St. Francis Inn has accumulated several time-honored ghost stories, mainly about Lily and her soldier lover who are said to make their rounds from time to time. The many paranormal events that have taken place for at least 160 years have usually indicated a classic haunting, as well as assorted poltergeist activity. There have been many reports of doors slamming throughout the day when no one is at the inn, as well as lights flickering, sometimes going on and off by themselves. Once, a visiting gentleman woke up from a deep sleep to find himself under his bed, wedged beneath the frame. He was so tightly wedged, in fact, that the St. Augustine Fire Department had to be called to set him free. Needless to say, the firemen were not the only people who were a little baffled, and most who heard of the strange event simply blamed the incident on the ghost of Lily, also known as the prankster of the St. Francis Inn.

Other common reports of supernatural occurrences involve poltergeist behavior. Apparently, objects are sometimes hurled across rooms, sometimes making such a racket—and a mess—that some of the inn's maids will refuse to work there alone. Once, the contents of a lady's handbag were thrown all over her room. Thinking that it just fell off her bed, she let the event go as an accident, but when her handbag was found full of water the next morning, she left the St. Francis in a hurry. In addition to those ghostly events, television sets will sometimes go on and off by themselves, and radios will be found turned on by themselves, and even changing stations while the witness just watches. Although some of the St. Francis's patrons have left in the middle of the night when the occurrences got a little too weird, for the most part these uncanny activities reflect a playful nature rather than one of harmful intent.

One of the reasons most paranormal researchers believe the activity is caused by Lily is that there have been reports of a ghostly, disembodied hand seen descending the rail of a staircase that once led down to the servants quarters. The hand is slender, feminine, and dark. Lily was said to be affectionate and good-natured in life, so it stands to reason that the predominantly harmless spirit at the St. Francis is hers. However, some believe there are still other spirits wandering this charming inn.

The soldier who took his own life in an upstairs room is also said to walk the grounds of the St. Francis, sometimes gazing out one of the third-floor windows. The soldier is reported to have an extremely sad demeanor to him, melancholy and distant, as if looking for something or someone. It stands to reason that he searches even today for his beloved Lily, though most psychics who have visited the St. Francis believe the two spirits have not met in the afterlife, for some reason, within the inn they both haunt.

Afterthoughts

St. Augustine is not shy on bed and breakfasts, and if you plan to visit this city as often as I do, the best thing to do is experience them all, one by one. I have been fortunate enough to have stayed at the St. Francis on several occasions, and every time, I have had a wonderful experience.

Although I have not experienced any out-and-out ghostly activity, my girlfriend woke up on several occasions with the feeling of someone standing over her, while I was fast asleep. She said that when she had overpowering feelings of being watched, she would open her eyes slowly, fixing them on a dark figure standing toward the foot of her side of the bed. She would reach over to make sure it was not me standing there, and then she naturally became a little concerned. After she finally got enough nerve to turn on the light, the image, a distinct human figure, would be gone, only a blank wall in its place. Now, it's possible that she imagined the whole affair, but when we woke up late that morning, the light next to her and the bathroom light were both turned on. Either one of us was sleepwalking, or we had a playful guest in our room while we slept. Although this might be a little unnerving for most, we never felt threatened by our nighttime caller.

17

Casa de la Paz

The Waiting Bride

A Little History

The beautiful Mediterranean-style Casa de la Paz has a long and illustrious history. Built for use as a private residence during the Flagler era, the building was also a beautiful bed and breakfast for several years, and will fondly be remembered as one of St. Augustine's most beloved inns. The Casa de la Paz Bayfront Bed & Breakfast offered beautiful rooms with a quintessential charm, and the innkeepers made sure that their guests received only the best attention during their stay, whether the occasion was a romantic getaway for two or a family engagement. The building is within walking distance of the Castillo de San Marcos, the Bridge of Lions, and many of the fine restaurants and cafés in the nation's oldest city.

The original owner in 1915 was J. Duncan Puller, who used the Casa de la Paz strictly as a private residence. Later, the house served as a small apartment building until the late 1970s, then underwent renovation in the mid-1980s to become a bed and breakfast. Today, this beautiful home, which graces St. Augustine's bayfront and historic district overlooking the sparkling Matanzas Bay, is once again a private residence.

Formerly the Casa de la Paz Bed &Breakfast, the house is now a private residence once again.

In its heyday, the accommodations were luxurious and gracious, with each of the seven rooms romantically distinctive, reminiscent of the early 1900s. Some of the rooms had spectacular views of the Bay and the Bridge of Lions, as well as the famous black-and-white striped lighthouse, while other rooms overlooked gorgeous Spanish-styled gardens in the rear courtyard. But one thing is for sure: as a guest, you were bound to have a wonderful time. Indeed, guests came to know why the name Casa de la Paz literally means "House of Peace," as their rest and relaxation was guaranteed in this Flagler-age B&B. However, the house seems to be home to at least one distressed spirit that refuses to rest and relax—the spirit of the morose bride.

Although there's little known about this landmark's past, there was one incident from the time of the original owner that is remembered today through the spirit of a young lady known as "the waiting lady." Though there seem to be two versions of this ghost story, most agree that the following legend is the truth, while the other is more romantic fantasy.

The first version tells of three women who were staying at the inn on vacation during the early 1900s. Two of the women left to return home and the last woman stayed, but soon after she became ill. Suffering from a fever the night before she had planned to leave, she died in her sleep. After the event, her spirit is said to wander the second floor, primarily on the top landing of the staircase. She has been heard saying, "Is it time to leave. . . Is it time to leave yet?" It is surely a sad story, as this spirit does not seem to be able to leave the lovely inn.

The second version, and by far the more romantic, tells us that this spirit in residence had come to the home many years ago on her honeymoon as a guest of the Puller family. As the story goes, she and her new husband had stayed for some time on holiday there and were preparing to leave after their pleasant stay. It was on the couple's last day in St. Augustine when the husband, a young vital man, decided to take a small boat out to go fishing—one last indulgence before he had to leave. He told his young wife to pack their belongings and to relax in the gardens until he returned. He promised to return soon.

The couple had been married for such a short time and their love, although equally young, was strong. The woman packed the suitcases for their trip back north, then sat in the gardens with a cup of tea. Even though the gardens were comforting and the tea delightful, she could not overcome a dreadful feeling, a feeling of doom. The young bride wasn't wrong in her premonition, as a terrible storm arose suddenly that day, the winds blowing hard enough to topple the planters on the front porch, sending down blinding sheets of cold, stinging rain. The young lady stood at the front window in agony as she waited for her beloved husband to return . . . but he never did.

The storm was in fact so strong that late summer day that it capsized his boat, tossing the young man into the sea, never to be found. Although the small wooden boat washed ashore a few days later at Atlantic Beach, the man's body was never recovered.

The young lady is said to have changed that day after the storm, as she waited by the front door, suitcases packed and ready to go, hoping that her love would come through the door and take her in his arms. Tragically, this was not to be, and she was so wounded by this that she remained in St. Augustine for the rest of her life, always waiting for the man she loved. She is said to have grown old long before her time, literally willing herself to death. To this day, she has not left the house.

Ghostly Legends and Haunted Folklore

When the home was used as apartments in the 1960s, many of the tenants reported hearing a knock on the door, and a woman's sad voice echoing, "Is it time to leave yet?" Many have heard a door shut, and some have claimed to see a small foggy figure walking down the hall, then disappearing. On rare occasions when the spirit is completely visible, she may be seen at the top of the stairs, holding her brocade satchels, bags packed and ready to depart. Although there are few who have seen her face, the ones who have claimed that her face was covered in a veil of shadow with only the slightest outline of a sad expression belonging to a very young woman. Many say that you know she's near when you have a feeling that someone is behind you, or when you feel a cold gust of wind on the stairs. Many who have witnessed this sad spirit claimed to smell the scent of an old perfume, like violets or primrose.

Although the spirit has always lamented on wanting to leave the stately residence, she has never made it home. The farthest the sad specter has gotten is one flight downstairs to the music room. There, she is said to have been seen standing and looking around silently, then, from time to time, she will be seen playing with a small music box that sits on a table, which then begins to play seemingly on its own accord.

On other occasions, the guests, as well as the innkeepers, would hear the music box playing by itself at various hours of the day or night. The inn's family pet saw the sad, ghostly lady as well. Apparently, the innkeeper's old cat was sometimes seen looking at something in the air, and then tracking this unseen thing as if someone were passing from one room to another. The old cat tracked this phantom with a curious expression, cocking its head in disbelief, then going back to sleep as if it were just another guest—a guest whose had the longest stay in the Casa de la Paz's history.

Paranormal researchers have maintained a common belief that animals and young children will be able to see certain things that most of us cannot, or choose not to see. This might be because animals and children see with an untrained eye, an innocent sense of perception, but as we get older we are literally trained not to believe in such things. Children and animals see what is there, pure and simple. Even the great British psychical researcher Harry Price would take his dog with him when exploring alleged haunted houses or buildings. He believed that the dog would respond to things he himself couldn't see, and sure enough, his canine companion would sometimes shudder with fright, or begin to wag its tail while staring at some unseen thing.

The haunting at the Casa de la Paz has been classified by some as a residual haunting, in which the ghostly image repeats itself over and over again, conducting the same behaviors in an "instant replay" manner. However this particular specter is able to break from a singular set of actions, playing with the music box for instance, and such actions only broaden the mystery of the sad guest who refuses to go home. Because these actions are differentiated as they are, many paranormal investigators believe that the spirit here may exist beyond a residual haunting, exhibiting more or less sentient behavior. The melancholy lady of the Casa de la Paz will no doubt remain as time-honored as this stately old residence . . . together forever throughout history.

Afterthoughts

The lady on the stairs is said still to walk during the wee hours of the night and morning, perpetually lost in an ether of sadness that she refuses to, or cannot depart from. Although many have considered using an exorcist on this poor soul, others are content with her presence as it is. When visiting the Casa de la Paz, remember that it is now a private residence, and no longer functioning as a bed and breakfast, so be sure to show the proper respects. While at one time guests of the inn enjoyed the quaint residence, the antique furnishings, and the charming atmosphere, even today you can always stand outside on the bay front and scan the home's dark windows after night has fallen. And though entering this beautiful home is not longer an option for most, you can still keep an ear open for the echoing music box chiming from the music room. If you do, don't be too surprised if you hear a disembodied voice of a slight woman asking you "Is it time to leave yet?" It might just be the waiting bride of the Casa de la Paz.

18

Casablanca Inn

A Light in the Window

A Little History

The beautifully restored Casablanca Inn is a fine example of St. Augustine's turn-of-the-century charm. The whitewash façade and its colonial columns are typical of St. Augustine's Flagler period, providing a timeless allure for its guests today.

Before it was the Casablanca Inn, it was known as the Matanzas Hotel. Following that, it became a boarding home called the Bayfront Boarding House. During the Prohibition era of the 1920s, bootleggers and rumrunners from the Caribbean would cruise Florida's shores selling their bootlegged liquor to happy customers from Miami to Mayport. The then-boarding house was owned and operated by an elderly widow, who, after many hardships and money problems, had a crazy idea that might save her—she decided she would help the bootleggers.

She earned money in two ways: first, she would work with the bootleggers to provide liquor to her guests and the locals; second, she would warn the bootleggers if federal agents were nearby or staying at the hotel. As these Treasury agents (or T-Men) frequently stayed at the

boarding house, she had the opportunity to warn the bootleggers before they came to shore. Thus her plan was accepted, and she became rich in only a short time.

History tells us that she would wait until after dark, then climb the stairs to the widow's walk. There, she would swing a lantern from left to right, signaling the bootleggers not to come ashore because the T-men were waiting. Her plan worked—she was well trusted and paid handsomely for her efforts. The rumrunners ended up establishing a speakeasy in her boarding house, selling rum and whisky to the guests and locals, which became a lucrative business.

This industrious woman made millions thanks to Prohibition. Although drinking alcohol was considered a crime back then, she did not feel that it was a sin and had vision enough to know that Prohibition would not last. By 1933, the lady had amassed a fortune and lived happily for many years.

She is buried in the Huguenot Cemetery, thought to be resting peacefully, but some believe she is reliving her glory days of evading Federal agents and warning the bootleggers of long ago. She is said to be swinging her lantern from the widow's walk even to this day.

Ghostly Legends and Haunted Folklore

The Casablanca Inn, much like its neighbors throughout St. Augustine, appears to be quite haunted. Of the most prevalent paranormal events to take place there is the sight of a dim lantern swaying from the widow's walk on the bed and breakfast's roof, seen especially by those out at sea or in the harbor. Countless mariners have called in to report that someone is in trouble at the Casablanca, thinking the light must be a call for assistance, but when someone goes there to investigate, no one is ever found.

The enterprising ghost has been known to appear throughout the Casablanca as well, and many guests over the years have reported seeing an apparition in the hallways and on the stairs. This ghostly image seems to be made of a foglike substance, which dissolves soon after being witnessed. Several of the guests over the years have reported feeling cold spots in their rooms. Some have complained that personal items have disappeared from their suitcases, only to find them again in the strangest of places, like on the balcony of the second floor or in the downstairs dining room right before they check out.

The lady's spirit has also been witnessed pacing on the roof on occasion, as if in contemplation. Many believe she continues her warning vigil to the seafaring bootleggers of the past, still alerting phantom vessels that treasury agents are nearby. Today shrimpers and other fisherman passing through the inlet may see a light swinging back and forth from the top of the inn. Moreover, those sleeping at the Casa de la Paz next door may be awakened by a light from the

Casablanca's roof shining into their windows.

Whether the lantern-swinging ghost lady is simply reenacting old behaviors or has been condemned for aiding and abetting felons is up to the believer. Although she remains an elusive spirit most of the time, her lantern is often witnessed by St. Augustine's locals, swinging from left to right on top of the Casablanca Inn.

Afterthoughts

Is the Casablanca haunted? Many seem to think so. Though this enterprising spirit is said to continue her endeavors in death as she had done in life, she is a reclusive ghost nonetheless. When visiting St. Augustine, try looking for the eerie light during foggy nights or heavy rains.

The Casablanca Inn is located at 24 Avenida Menendez, St. Augustine, Florida, 32084. For information, call 904-829-0928.

19

Harry's Seafood Bar and Grille

Catalina's Still Here

A Little History

The original structure that is now Harry's Seafood Bar and Grille, formerly Catalina's Garden Restaurant, dates back to at least around 1720, but is probably much older. The de Porras family had a child named Catalina in 1753, who would ultimately become the restaurant's namesake. The family lived in the house until the 1760s, when the Spanish surrendered control of Florida over to the British. The de Porras family would sail for Havana, Cuba, vowing never to return. Catalina, however, had other plans.

A decade passed and Catalina married Joseph Xavier Ponce de Leon. In 1784, Spain was taking possession of Florida once again, which opened up many opportunities for many Spaniards to return to the homes they had to abandon when the British took control years earlier. Seizing the opportunity, Catalina decided to return to St. Augustine with her husband. They returned with high hopes of moving back into the house she had always loved.

During the twenty-year British occupation, the house had remained unoccupied, save a storage house used by the military. After

a few years of negotiating, Catalina and Joseph finally got the house back with the governor's blessings in 1789. Catalina was happy, and began to settle in to make a home for her family. Sadly, however, Catalina would die only a few years after returning to St. Augustine. To make matters worse, a devastating fire swept through a good portion of St. Augustine's bayfront area in 1887, destroying the house. Fortunately however, sketches had been made of Catalina's house in the 1840s, and a replica of the lost home was rebuilt from those sketches in 1888, just as charming as the original.

The home served as an apartment building and boarding house for many years until becoming the Puerta Verde Restaurant in the

1970s. In 1985, it changed management to become the Chart House Restaurant, then changing again in 1993 to Catalina's Garden Restaurant. In 1997, the restaurant had once more been renamed to Harry's of St. Augustine, a fine eating and drinking establishment. But who is Harry anyway?

According to the restaurant's owners, and local legend, Harry is a horse.

Supposedly, the original owners of Harry's made a trip to New Orleans for Mardi Gras. While on holiday, they enjoyed the finest foods and were inspired to open a restaurant with food and atmosphere like the restaurants in New Orleans. It all seemed like a good idea until they looked in their empty wallets. They had to think of something, so they decided to go to the races and take a chance.

They found "Harry the Horse" listed at fifty-to-one odds, took a risk, and Harry wound up winning! They took their winnings and created Harry's, one of my favorite haunts when visiting St. Augustine. You will find very good food at Harry's, as well as libations and a festive atmosphere to boot. And, although most of the visitors will come to know Harry's just as a good place to eat, drink, and relax, most of the locals and employees know of another kind of spirit lurking in the restaurant. . . .

Ghostly Legends and Haunted Folklore

The haunting activities at Harry's vary from strange noises in the night to odd scents in empty rooms, but the most frequent report is a woman seen out of the corner of the eye. Although many feel this spirit is of a woman believed to have died in the fire of 1887, others believe it is the gentle ghost of Catalina herself.

The former owners and employees of all this restaurant's incarnations have reported the ephemeral vision of a young woman dressed in a white nightgown or dress just crossing their sight during the night hours, as if walking swiftly to another room. The witnesses would usually spot this fleeting phantom on the second floor, but she has been felt throughout the restaurant, especially in the ladies' restroom upstairs, where the image of what many feel is the spirit of Catalina will sometimes appear in a mirror.

Other paranormal activity to take place throughout the restaurant over the years includes strange, misplaced smells, like a woman's perfume, on the second floor or near the ladies restroom. Also, there has been what appears to be poltergeist activity in the restaurant: light switches will be turned off while the staff is working, and utensils and other objects will sometimes be found scattered all over the floor. But the most bizarre happenings are the spontaneous fires.

Back when Harry's was Catalina's Garden Restaurant, a series of strange fires started in the kitchen area seemingly by unseen hands. Apparently, when an employee was doing laundry and chores in the kitchen, she detected the faint scent of something burning, and when looking around for a fire, she was startled to see the laundry basket next to her smoldering, soon becoming a small fire. Understandably, startled, she put the fire out and inspected the area to see why the still partially damp laundry would catch fire. As there were no signs of flammable chemicals or cigarettes near the basket, the whole affair soon became the city's newest ghostly mystery.

These small but eerie fires continued on rare occasions for a few years following the basket fire, and fortunately, there haven't been any outbreaks for quite some time. Many have attributed these fires to one of the victims of the 1887 fire, which had destroyed many of the homes on St. Augustine's bayfront. This victim, although she remains largely a mystery—to some only a fable—was a woman named Bridgett. Legend tells us she may have been sleeping in the second-floor bedroom when it began to burn, waking too late to escape the flames. After this woman died, many of the neighbors said that they saw an eerie glowing light go on where her bedroom once was, then it would go off by itself. This phenomenon was reported on several occasions during the weeks after the fire, but soon subsided, then ceased altogether.

Today, although there are fewer paranormal incidents, there are some who claim the restaurant is still quite haunted. Psychics and ghost hunters have come to Harry's in hopes of finding the spirits of either Catalina or the mysterious Bridgett. Some have gone away empty-handed, but a select few have gone home knowing that there is something more to this lively little restaurant. Some have seen images in the ladies' restroom mirror, or have detected the light scent of perfume from another age, and still some have caught the fleeting image of a vaporous woman walking past them.

Is Harry's haunted? As with the majority of St. Augustine's establishments and landmarks, I would have to say yes. Perhaps the sounds and even the strange scents may be a result of something quite ordinary, perhaps something totally logical in explanation, but the locals of this ancient city will most likely think otherwise.

Afterthoughts

Harry's Seafood Bar and Grille is delightful, and should be visited when you're in St. Augustine. I make it a habit to stop in when on business or just going shopping in the ancient city. Although I have yet to catch Catalina sneaking past me, or detect her sweet perfume, I feel that there is indeed something here. If you're looking for spirits at Harry's, I suggest going in the evenings, just before closing. Catalina or Bridgett, whoever haunts this restaurant, is believed to make her appearances in the nighttime when it's quiet.

Harry's Seafood Bar & Grille is located at 46 Avenida Menendez, St. Augustine, Florida, 32084. For information, call 904-824-7765.

20

The Florida School for the Deaf and the Blind

The Little Boy with Blond Hair

A Little History

Throughout my travels in this great state of Florida collecting ghost stories and haunted folk tales, I have heard many indeed. In St. Augustine I discovered a real cache of such stories and legends. From old forts to charming bed and breakfasts, I have investigated and visited them all, but one particular legend in that cache spooked me the most. It wasn't a story about the old fort, which has seen more than its share of pain and death, or the old Spanish hospital, which has most likely seen just as much carnage. No, this particular legend, albeit a somewhat hidden one, takes place in a school for special children, in a peaceful, majestic section of a residential neighborhood.

The Florida School for the Deaf and the Blind is a state-supported boarding school for hearing- and visually impaired children from pre-school through the twelfth grade. It was founded in 1885 and has a seventy-acre campus in the north section of St. Augustine, just before the bridge to Vilano Beach, right on the Intracoastal Waterway. The buildings represent many eras of the school's history, from 1885 to the present day. The distinctive red-tile roofs and courtyards accentuated by lush palms and live oak trees with hanging moss give one a feeling of the gentle nature of the Old South.

Today, the Florida School for the Deaf and the Blind is the largest school of its kind in America. Beginning with three small schoolhouses, it is now more than forty buildings and is not only well accepted, but is greatly appreciated by these special children and their parents who hail from all across the country. Although many have come and gone over the years, some of the old students or others unknown are believed to have remained, and among them is the little boy with blond hair.

Ghostly Legends and Haunted Folklore

Although many of the children who have come here over the years have graduated and gone on to higher education and happy lives, one poor soul is said still to wander the school for reasons unknown. This spectral child, whoever he might have been in life, is an unpleasant entity indeed.

This ghostly figure is said to roam the restrooms on the east wing of the first floor. He is described as a teenage boy dressed in old-fashioned clothes from around the early 1900s. The frightening specter has been seen by several of the deaf female students in the restroom at night, and many of these girls are said to have run to the teachers, screaming for dear life. Apparently, this very frightening specter is seen suspended from either a shower rod or light fixture on the wall of the girls' restroom. His neck is said to be cut almost completely off. Apparently, this horrible specter then gets down from the rod or fixture and shambles with a trail of blood flowing from him, walks into a wall, then simply vanishes.

If this image isn't frightening enough, this specter is also said to be laughing with a high-pitched voice and gargling, as if choking on his own blood. As the boy vanishes into the adjacent wall, a huge gust of wind will begin to blow. Then, the doors slam shut, the lights go out, and the poor witnesses see a pair of glowing red eyes. Moreover, as soon as the high-pitched laughter begins again, the lights go back on, leaving the helpless victim to bolt out of that bathroom in a trail of screams and tears.

This boy with blond hair, although seemingly evidence of an evil murder, seems to have eluded history. After careful research, I have found no evidence of a murder reported on the premises of the school. Judging by the reports of this spirit's clothing, he could have been living anytime between the 1860s and the 1900s, making it a possibility that he was murdered on this spot before the school was built in the 1880s. Although this particular specter is more than enough for any haunted location, the school appears to have several other apparitions that have been seen on campus. These apparitions have been reported for years by both the children and the staff of the school—heard by the blind and seen by the deaf. Along with other paranormal events, such as strange odors, misplaced noises, and cold spots, the Florida School for the Deaf and the Blind appears to be a spirited place indeed.

Afterthoughts

This particular story seems to have all the earmarks of the classic student-to-student ghost story, which becomes a rite of passage that can be found at almost any school. Indeed, as I went to a military school during my high school years, I can still remember the stories of the ghostly cadet who was accidentally shot and killed on the rifle range almost one hundred years ago. I can remember the legend of how this unfortunate cadet would walk around in the chapel and throughout the school building that was named for him. Although I never saw the phantom cadet, many students over the years have claimed to be eyewitnesses.

It's important to weigh such stories, as with all the stories told herein, with a good amount of skeptical inquiry. In the case of the children reporting such nightmarish creatures, they may indeed be the results of active imaginations rather than true ghosts. After all, what room full of kids, a little frightened from being away from home, would not tell a ghost story or two when tucked in for bed at night? It's only natural for young and active imaginations to supplement a little after hearing such urban legends. Is there a horrific ghost haunting the restrooms of this school? Maybe, but it's a good bet this spirit has been embellished just a little bit. You'll have to use the facilities yourself at this school to know for sure.

21

Huguenot Cemetery

St. Augustine's Most Haunted Graveyard

A Little History

The Huguenot Cemetery is an essential site of interest in the ancient city, and indeed, this cemetery holds more than its share of historical figures, and many believe it holds more than its share of ghosts, too. The Huguenot Cemetery, one of St. Augustine's original "Publik Burying Grounds" became well used when a yellow fever epidemic hit in 1821, not long after Florida became a U. S. territory. The name "Huguenot" refers to the French adventurers and explorers, specifically those of Protestant faiths, which made up a small denomination in the city.

The Huguenot Cemetery officially opened after the yellow fever epidemic ravaged St. Augustine, marking the burial of hundreds of victims and hundreds more in unmarked graves. The Huguenot Cemetery was used until the summer of 1884 and is today kept by the city's First Presbyterian Church. Although visitors to St. Augustine will no doubt see this cemetery as a quaint, antique graveyard, many of the locals recognize the Huguenot as a final refuge after many a horrific event in their city's past.

As with most places in St. Augustine, the Huguenot Cemetery has its share of restless spirits and haunted legends, and there isn't one ghost tour in the ancient city that overlooks the story of Judge John B. Stickney and the plight of his earthly remains. His story is more than that of a ghostly visitor in search of something; it's a story that warns the living not to disturb or show disrespect to the dead under any circumstances. In other words, let buried bones lie.

Ghostly Legends and Haunted Folklore

The Huguenot Cemetery, surrounded by a brick wall and a black iron fence, amid huge oak trees adorned with low-hanging Spanish moss, has a look usually associated with hauntings. And it would be an injustice for such an atmospheric location not to have at least one good ghost story attached to it. Indeed, the Huguenot has its share of stories. Many claim to see the spirits of little children sitting on the posts and walls of this monument, as well as on the tombstones within—most likely the victims of yellow fever, many of whom are believed to have been buried in mass graves. Little Elisabeth, the young spirit who has been witnessed dancing around the old city gates just east of the cemetery, has also been seen near the Huguenot's walls in the dead of night. In addition, though these spirits are certainly spooky to behold, one particular ghost outshines them all—the ghost of Judge John B. Stickney.

Judge Stickney, a widower with three small children, moved to St. Augustine shortly after the Civil War. The judge lived in the city until he died of typhoid fever in 1882 while visiting Washington, D. C. At the request of his last will and testament, his body was returned to St. Augustine for burial in the Huguenot Cemetery. In 1903, after his children had moved to Washington, they decided to have his body moved and reburied closer to them.

Late one evening, while the gravediggers were in the process of exhuming the remains of Judge Stickney, two drunken men chased the gravediggers away before the exhumation was complete. The judge's coffin was molding and caving in from decay, and so exposed his skeletal remains. The sight of these remains was nothing new to these two drunkards, as they had been in the business of grave robbing on many occasions before, and they decided to have a look for something of value. Sure enough, the judge's gold-filled teeth shined like a beacon when the grave robbers held their lantern over the coffin. Within a few seconds the men had pried the gold teeth out with their knives, and along they went with one of the best hauls they'd had in years. But apparently, the judge did not like this.

When the gravediggers returned with the authorities, they found the opened coffin and most of the judge's remains, but in the process of the robbery the skull had fallen away from the rest of the skeleton. Many legends surfaced that these grave robbers were found dead a short time latter, but most of St. Augustine's historians feel this is merely an urban legend to frighten off potential grave robbers. Although that tidbit of history may have been fabricated, another legend reports that Judge Stickney has returned from the grave to seek out his gold teeth.

Reportedly, Judge Stickney has been seen walking through the Huguenot Cemetery, complete in his burial regalia consisting of a black top hat and flowing black cape. The judge is almost always observed looking around the corners of tombstones and monuments, always with a determined look, a look of disgust and anger. Sometimes, the judge is seen without a head, nothing more than a dark, caped figure passing the graves like smoke. Other times, witnesses spot the judge sitting on a low-hanging branch of one of the old oak trees, right over the spot of his original grave.

Although most who witness this determined spirit see him actively searching for something, some claimed to have seen a headless man wandering through the cemetery aimlessly. Though the skull of Judge Stickney was said to have been removed by the grave robbers, we have to remember that these shameless thieves might have been disrespectful to more than the judge alone. As gold teeth were certainly a common dental procedure in the 1800s, it is likely there were more victims over the years, victims who might also be haunting this cemetery. Perhaps there is indeed more than one vengeful spirit lurking around the tombstones and trees of this ancient burial ground. Perhaps Judge Stickney has ghostly company. This would seem to make sense, as the Huguenot Cemetery is considered to be one of the most haunted sites in St. Augustine.

Afterthoughts

The Huguenot Cemetery is usually open during the morning hours, and with special permission from the historical society, tours may be provided. Although the cemetery is always locked and off-limits in the evening, visitors can still take photos over the low walls surrounding the area. There is ample light there, and it is only footsteps from the old city gates and directly across the street from the Castillo de San Marcos.

The Huguenot Cemetery has attracted many paranormal investigators over the years, and many have gone away with the evidence they had hoped for. Many ghost hunters have been able to capture strange images in their photographs while exploring late at night. Some have caught the ever-mysterious orbs floating throughout the inner circumference of the cemetery, and on occasion, they've also seen shapes of people and human faces within the bark of the trees. The cemetery seems to hold many spirits, both tortured and seemingly enlightened.

The Huguenot Cemetery is a must-see when visiting St. Augustine. Enjoy the sights of the ancient city, the shopping, the dining, and all of the city's unique offerings. Enjoy the history this city holds within its antediluvian boundaries, but absolutely never take gold teeth from a grave . . . someone or something might just come after them.

22

The Old Jail

Dexter

A Little History

Constructed in 1891 by Henry Flagler, this jail was created because the first jail in St. Augustine sat directly across from the Hotel Ponce de Leon, Flagler's magnificent creation. Because a jail would no doubt be offensive to his high-class clientele, Flagler relocated the facility to north of the city on San Marco Street. He donated all the materials and paid for the new jailhouse and an adjacent building, which later became the sheriff's lodging. This jail was in operation for more than sixty years, and is one of the few surviving nineteenth-century jails in America today, and of course it's no surprise that it's in St. Augustine.

Inside, visitors will see the original sheriff's office and domicile, the male and female jail cells, the maximum-security area, and an impressive collection of weapons used over the years. Prisoners last stayed there in the 1950s; then the building was used for storage for the city, and then it became an attraction for visitors. Although the many prisoners that stayed in this jail over the years may not have been notorious or infamous—most were petty thieves or drunk drivers—some of them were quite dangerous. Because accessing the records of these criminals is almost impossible, we must rely on oral traditions and local legends.

Ghostly Legends and Haunted Folklore

One legend revolves around a man, a flim-flam man if you will, whom some have called Dexter. Now, no one is quite sure what his full name was, or where exactly he came from, but several people I spoke to during my investigations told me that during the late 1920s there was a man matching Dexter's description. This man was caught pilfering jewelry from unsuspecting women at the Hotel Ponce de Leon, as well as swindling others in town by selling phony stocks and bonds. But Dexter wasn't as smooth as he thought he was.

When he was investigated by the city constable, jewelry and other assorted tidbits of evidence were found in his possession, and he was quickly jailed. According to local legend, a few of the husbands of the women he robbed were less than forgiving, and death threats were made. Dexter was a lean man, and certainly not a fighter. He made his living by going from town to town, running a quick scam, then moving on to the next town.

Perhaps this was the first time Dexter was apprehended, or perhaps the nature of the threats was just too frightening for the wiry thief. With the terrorization from outside his jail cell and browbeating from the sheriff, Dexter died in his sleep and was found the next morning, balled up on his narrow wall cot.

Many, if not all of the prisoners over the years wore the mandatory prison garb—gray-and-black-striped coveralls—and there's no doubt Dexter wore the same outfit during his brief stay in the old jail. In his prime, however, he was said to be fond of wearing a brown-and-tan plaid suit, along with his gold pocket watch and bowler hat. He thought himself quite debonair, even though that did not save him from the law or his own guilty heart.

To this day, many tour guides and tourists alike have seen the faint image of a gaunt man standing in the main cell block, wearing a plaid suit, and holding a small round hat in his hands. The ghost is said to look sad and remorseful, as if standing in front of a judge, hoping for exoneration. The "man in plaid" is sometimes heard shuffling his feet, usually in the locked cells. When you look back to where the sounds came from, you'll most likely find nothing, just empty, dark space. Dexter is indeed a sad specter; although most have forgotten his illicit deeds in life, he apparently has not.

In addition to Dexter, some have seen the shadowy shape of a tall man on the walls, and several of the employees feel it is the ghost of the first sheriff at the jailhouse, Sheriff Perry. Perry was said to have been well over 6'5" and very sturdy in stature.

From time to time, people notice a putrid, sweaty smell. Because the sanitary facilities for the prisoners consisted of one bucket of cold, soapy water, some believe that these prisoners continue to emit an unwashed aroma in the afterlife just as they did in life. Cold spots are also quite common throughout the cells and sheriff's office, even in the extreme heat of summer.

Afterthoughts

The old jail seems to have more than its share of paranormal activity, so much so that there have been many psychics and paranormal investigators who claim that the entire jail is active with both benign and malevolent spirits. So, when visiting the old jail, stay aware of the cold spots that appear out of nowhere, keep an eye open for a tall shadow on the cell walls, and above all, try to remember poor Dexter. When walking past the main cellblock, you might want to whisper, "We forgive you, Dexter," remembering the torment and guilt that followed him to his grave.

23
The St. Augustine Lighthouse

The Enchanted Lighthouse

A Little History

The St. Augustine Lighthouse is one more haunted location on our tour, and the last in Florida's ghostly journey. The lighthouse is considered by many paranormal researchers to be one of the most haunted sites in Florida, and with good reason. Because there have been many deaths, suicides, and executions there over the years, the St. Augustine Lighthouse appears to attract more than just ships at sea.

Although there has been a signal of some sort on this site since the 1500s—a 40-foot watch tower with flags and a lamp—a more modern lighthouse would not be constructed until 1824. This wood and stone structure was Florida's first lighthouse. Construction on the current tower began in 1871, and was designed by Paul Pelz, an architect involved in designing the Library of Congress in Washington, D. C. Constructed of southern red brick, granite, and iron, the new lighthouse was finished on October 15, 1874. Now one of the tallest lighthouses in the United States, it takes 227 steps to climb to the top where there is the tower's light and a magnificent view of the ancient city.

The lighthouse keeper's home, a red brick Victorian house designed to serve as many as three lighthouse keepers and their families at one time, was completed in 1876. This spacious home has a large dining room and tea parlor on the first floor and several bedrooms on the second floor. The storage compartments and cisterns, which are man-made reservoirs designed for collecting water for the home, are located in the basement. It was altogether a highly advanced lighthouse station and living quarters for those days. By the turn of the century, summer kitchens and indoor plumbing were installed throughout the lighthouse station, and by 1925, the home was equipped with electric lights, bringing the lighthouse to its modern state of operation.

The St. Augustine Lighthouse was one of the first to have a Fresnel lens and an operating system constructed of four concentric wicks burning oil made from pig fat. In 1936, after many years of fuel-efficient service, the lighthouse changed from pig fat to kerosene, to adapt for electricity, which made the lens rotate with quick, thirty-second flashes. It represented yet another jump in maritime progress.

In 1955, the lighthouse became completely automated, and the lighthouse keepers were no longer needed, thus ending a long tradition of maritime service. By the 1960s, the lighthouse was boarded up and abandoned, except for a skeleton maintenance crew. A few years later, in 1971, someone set fire to the lighthouse and the adjoining home. The tower was spared, but the interior of the beautiful Victorian home was destroyed, leaving only its blackened brick exterior.

It wasn't long after this event, however, that St. Johns County purchased the lighthouse's remains and began a restoration project. Today, the St. Augustine Lighthouse and the Victorian home serve as a historical museum. It is open to the public seven days a week and has a guided tour throughout the grounds. And yes, it even has a ghost tour.

Although its history appears rather typical, there is indeed much more to the past of this beautiful lighthouse than meets the eye. This location was the site of numerous pirate raids, and ultimately the place where those same pirates were hanged. There have been several deaths there—by accident, suicide, and maybe even murder, only the ghosts could tell for sure. But one thing is for certain, there's something downright frightening there.

Ghostly Legends and Haunted Folklore

The St. Augustine Lighthouse has had a spooky history practically since its inception. One of the most time-honored maritime legends tells us that lighthouses are believed to attract the souls of men lost at sea. These spirits are believed to follow the beacon of a lighthouse, so that it acts as a form of refuge for wandering spirits. The St. Augustine Lighthouse seems to be following this paranormal tradition, as it is reputedly haunted, and has been for at least 150 years.

I can remember hearing a story a few years ago when the museum was undergoing restorations. Apparently, a maintenance worker was moving various boxes and equipment. While in the process of picking up one end of a very heavy bench, moving it to one side, and stepping back to get a better perspective of where it should go, a strange feeling came over him, accompanied by a sudden cold draft. Ignoring the strange feeling, he walked around to the opposite end of the bench to move it. As he was beginning to do this, the bench went up in the air about two feet and began slowly to move by itself. Now, I don't know how the worker reacted initially, but he certainly did not return the next day.

Over the years, the lighthouse has attracted more than just wandering ghosts and paranormal researchers—film crews have come there to experience the lighthouse's ghostly legends. Several years ago, PBS sent film crews to the lighthouse to film a feature on lighthouses of America's Southeast. Not long after that, the Discovery Channel arrived to film a documentary on the spirits of America's lighthouses. The Discovery Channel's film crew went not only in search of the history of Florida's premier lighthouse, but also in search of its unique specters.

During the filming, several of the film crew reported a misty, grayish-colored man walking on the second floor of the Victorian home. They also reported feeling cold spots in areas where there could be no draft, or where there were no air conditioning vents, as well as the faint odor of cigar smoke where no smoke should be—the museum is a no-smoking environment. Moreover, the crew reported hearing strange noises, like shuffling feet on the stairs throughout the home and in the lighthouse. They even witnessed the lights flickering while climbing the lighthouse tower. The film crew is surely now convinced about the existence of ghosts.

Even though there are most likely dozens of spirits who haunt this beautiful lighthouse, to date there have been only three definite spirits reported. Although the history may be a little hazy, legend tells us that there was a young girl around ten or eleven years of age who was killed by a passing train in the early 1900s. This spirit is said to walk around the grounds, showing her presence through her footsteps on the gravel surrounding the lighthouse. And on rare occasions she is seen walking behind the dense bushes near the tower. She is a fleeting wisp of a spirit, and has proven to be benign in her actions. Only a select few have seen the faint image of a girl wearing the dress of the early twentieth century. But she's not the only little girl to haunt this lighthouse.

Another story revolving around spectral children tells of a tragic accident that resulted in the drowning deaths of two girls. Although I have heard two separate versions of their deaths, the first story tells us that the two daughters of the lighthouse's builder were playing on the seashore, swimming in the crashing surf, when either a strong wave or the undertow pulled the two girls under and drowned them. Many feel that this sad accident explains at least one of the little specters, yet others feel these girls died another way.

The second legend tells us that in the 1870s, while the two children of the lighthouse keeper and a young African-American child were playing on a railroad handcar, a terrible accident occurred. The handcar apparently went off the track and fell into the sea. While the friend escaped, the two unfortunate sisters were trapped under the heavy handcar and drowned.

Either way, there have been many reported sightings of a little girl looking out the windows of the lighthouse and sometimes waiting by the lighthouse keeper's door. In 1955, when the tower was first automated, several people rented the home. It wasn't long until they reported hearing strange things in the night, as well as seeing what they believed to be the ghost of a little girl wandering the hallways. Some believed that the little spirit was the daughter of Hezekiah Pittee, who supervised the building of the lighthouse in the 1870s.

There is another spirit who many feel is a man who hanged himself during the early 1930s. Though his name and the exact date of his suicide are hazy, he is believed to have been distraught after losing a fortune in the stock market crash of 1929. He is said to have wandered in off the beach where he had been living, walked into the old house, and promptly hanged himself in one last effort to escape his troubles. To this day, his specter is said to appear during stormy nights or when it is especially dark inside the house. The image of a hanged man is sometimes seen gently swaying from the wood rafter of the old home.

In 1985 when the old home was being refurbished, one of the workers in the garden claimed to have seen a man hanging inside. It was only after this event that the workers learned of the suicide that took place almost sixty years earlier. Other times when the men were working during the daylight hours, some would claim to get strange feelings, as if being watched, and sometimes they felt an icy cold wind descending over them. When they would look up and over their shoulders, they would see a man in faded overalls hanging from one of the rafters. Several of the workers signed off that particular job, leaving it to someone else. I can't really blame them for that.

Apparently, the renovations were stirring up more than just dust. Some of these workers, having to spend their nights in the old Victorian home because they had expensive equipment inside, often complained of odd things going on. The workers would wake up in the middle of the night saying that they had seen the shadowy image of a young girl in turn-of-the-century clothes. She was wearing a big bow on her head and a light-colored dress with a white apron. She would be standing over them, just staring down strangely. Understandably shaken, the men would stand up to see why a little girl would be standing in the old room in the first place, but as soon as they got to their feet, the child would take a few steps backward and simply vanish, right before their eyes. Sometimes, the workers would awake to the gentle humming of an innocent child.

But wait, that's not all. There are still a few spirits unaccounted for in this most haunted lighthouse. It seems that in the basement area below the old Victorian home there may be a few spirits roaming around. As if this lighthouse didn't already have enough spirits within it, many have reported seeing the misty image of a large man in the basement, or sometimes they get a strong feeling of dread in this area. Again, we have a mystery as to the proper identity of this particular spirit, or spirits, but nonetheless, the basement area of the lighthouse is undoubtedly one of the spookiest places in St. Augustine. As one lighthouse tour guide put it, "It's just too darn creepy down there."

Although the presence in the basement is believed by some to be one or two of the lighthouse's former caretakers, a few feel that the presence is of a darker nature. The first suspected identity is that of an unfortunate man who fell to his death while painting the upper portion of the tower in 1859. He fell over 160 feet, an unspeakable demise that might have anyone returning as a disgruntled ghost. Some, on the other hand, believe that the ghost in the basement may be the spirit of the first lighthouse keeper, who died mysteriously while hauling fuel up the winding stairs of the lighthouse. Although many think it was a heart attack, some have even suggested that he was murdered, making the legend of lighthouse even more bizarre. Still, others feel the uneasy atmosphere in the basement area comes from a much darker source. Indeed, this section of the basement has always appeared to be haunted. And, although the spirit or spirits in question have never been properly identified, almost everyone reports an uneasy feeling while down there alone.

Although no one is quite certain about the exact historical significance of this location, many paranormal investigators and historians believe that this is the site of a mass burial. Long before the new lighthouse and home were constructed, the old tower did the job of ushering the ships at sea to safety. During this period of Florida's history, pirates were an unfortunate reality. They would often sack the homes in St. Augustine and were guilty of other terrible crimes. However, on occasion, some these pirates were caught, and when a pirate was captured, he was certain to die on the gallows.

On one such occasion, thirteen pirates were apprehended, brought to a swift trial, and quickly hanged on the shores of St. Augustine beach. As per custom, they were buried behind the old lighthouse in a shallow grave. Now, no one knows for sure exactly where these scoundrels were buried, but some feel it is where the home now sits, or where the cisterns were dug. Perhaps the original workers did indeed find bones, but having little care for such things, they likely finished the job without ceremony.

Even though the basement area remains somewhat of a mystery to paranormal researchers, almost everyone agrees that this area of the lighthouse just feels wrong. There are very few who will not look over their shoulders when climbing the stairs, and there are even fewer who would volunteer to stay down there for the night. The basement section is undoubtedly the creepiest place throughout the lighthouse museum, especially at night.

Afterthoughts

The St. Augustine Lighthouse and Museum is a must-see locale when visiting the ancient city, where there's always more to a historical site than meets the eye. The guides at the lighthouse are more than happy to talk about their ghosts, and pleased to keep the legends alive.

There are certainly many reasons why the lighthouse and the surrounding area would be haunted. After all, with such tragedies as the little girl killed by a passing train and the handcar accident that killed more children, a lingering spirit would seem to make sense. The unhappy man who committed suicide in the lighthouse keeper's home and the unfortunate caretaker who fell to his death would certainly warrant a couple of sad spirits, too. And let's not forget the thirteen executed pirates buried behind the lighthouse. With such anger and spite, how could this place not be haunted?

If indeed a lighthouse could act as a beacon to draw in spirits, then the St. Augustine Lighthouse and Museum is certainly doing its share of populating this delightful city with the spirits of Florida's dead.

Paranormal researchers and psychics visiting the St. Augustine Lighthouse will find this area a particular delight, as it's a sure bet they won't leave empty-handed. Many researchers and ghost hunters have captured photographic anomalies such as orbs and tornado-like spectral images known as "vortexes." Moreover, many have also captured what they believe to be the voices of the dead, through electronic voice phenomena, EVP, in the basement section of the lighthouse keeper's home, as well as detecting other oddities while using various scientific gadgetry.

When visiting, be sure to bring your camera, for there's much to see here, but keep this in mind: As there are so many spirits reputedly haunting this area, don't be surprised if you bring someone or something home with you. After all, this is the most haunted city in the United States.

Ghost Tours of St. Augustine and the St. Augustine Lighthouse and Museum offer a ninety-minute tour with ghostly tales of the lighthouse's colorful past. The tour includes a walk through the historical Lighthouse Park and neighborhood, a trip to the lighthouse keeper's home, plus a climb to the top of the 165-foot tower. The museum is a working lighthouse with collections and assorted exhibitions that reflect St. Augustine's rich history, creating an entertaining and educational tour.

The St. Augustine Lighthouse and Museum is located at 81 Lighthouse Ave. For information call 904-829-0745.

Afterthoughts

The very name Florida most often conjures a tropical paradise where millions of Americans vacation each year to enjoy the climate, beaches, and the unique nature and hospitality Florida offers. But Florida must now also be seen in a very different light. And, knowing that these stories only represent a fraction of the many legends and historical accounts of Florida's supernatural events, let this modest collection be an invitation into the seldom-discussed world of Florida's unknown.

Over the years, I have been very fortunate to have heard some of the most fascinating ghost stories right here in the Sunshine State. As I journeyed throughout the state, I had the chance to visit some of the creepiest and also the most beautiful places imaginable. Places like the remains of Sunland Hospital in Tallahassee, which told of darker times in Florida's history. When I visited, its wrecked hulk sat as a reminder that we should respect those who cannot find peace in death, and as a symbol of the pain and sadness that occurred there so many years ago. Equally frightening, and still standing today, the decayed carcass of Jacksonville's School Four represents both the stately beauty of our state's educational past as well as the dim and sinister future it was soon to attain.

Indeed, such dark and foreboding places certainly filled me, and many other ghost hunters, with a sense of awe, amazement, and even a touch of fear. Yet, other locations like the Herlong Mansion Bed and Breakfast in Micanopy, the May-Stringer House Museum in Brooksville, and the Casa Marina Hotel on the shores of Jacksonville Beach are prime examples of the splendor Florida has to offer. Throughout my ghostly trek, I felt more than just the antiquity from these places, I truly sensed a silent enchantment, as if there were hints of life within these intriguing places.

When visiting St. Augustine, truly one of my most favorite spots in all of Florida, I cannot help looking over my shoulder at times. The ancient Castillo de San Marcos sits eloquently on the crisp waters off Anastasia Island and holds within it the fragrant memories of an equally ancient love affair. And what of the restless soldier that still walks the battlements, forever searching for something he lost more than 300 years ago? When I walk the magnificent hallways of Flagler College, I will always keep an eye open for the lady in blue, who sits in her solemn loneliness, waiting for the man she would love for an eternity. And what of the little boy who searches for a playmate? Does he still haunt this institution's silent corridors late at night? Indeed, this entire city appears to be haunted.

With what I experienced during my visits to some of Florida's allegedly haunted locations, whether old forgotten graveyards or fine hotels and bed and breakfasts, I definitely feel that the Sunshine State has more than its share of spirits and haunted settings. After all, there is so much more than the swampy marshlands, moss-covered oaks, and inviting beaches the postcards depict. Florida appears to have a wide variety of ghosts, spirits, haunts, and other things that go bump in the night.

When visiting Florida, be sure to enjoy the many conveniences our Sunshine State has to offer. Enjoy the amusement parks, the many fine restaurants, and the fast-paced nightspots, and don't forget to bring your suntan oil when relishing our magnificent beaches. Although you will enjoy Florida, don't be surprised if you experience the uncanny, the strange, or the supernatural. Happy ghost hunting!

Appendices

Appendix A

Tools of the Modern Ghost Hunter

The ghost hunter today, whether he or she is a highly educated scholar with a university grant to fund research, or the stout-of-heart amateur hoping to find evidence of life after death, has need of scientific equipment. Indeed, such equipment is as important as bravery when it comes to walking through deserted cemeteries in the dead of night, or when exploring the old, abandoned, reputedly haunted houses during a stormy evening. Having the proper equipment can make the difference between a successful ghost hunt and just another evening stroll.

There are only a few organizations and businesses that sell fascinating items like electromagnetic reading devices, remote motion sensors to smudge sticks for cleaning a haunted area, and even dowsing rods for finding a ghost. One of the best places to find these high-tech toys is at the Ghosthunter Store at www.ghosthunterstore.com. The following examples are tools used by many paranormal investigators in their research, and although many are expensive, most of these tools are quite common and available at many department stores today:

Air-Ion Counter: This is an expensive piece of equipment, and it is used to measure the amount of positive and negative ions in the area. Ghosts can cause a lot of positive ions because they give off high amounts of electromagnetic discharges.

Baby/Talcum Powder: Used in order to find evidence of ghostly footsteps or hand prints.

Barometer: Ghost hunters have used barometers to look for paranormal activity. Some investigators believe that some paranormal events can affect barometric pressure.

Batteries: You should always bring many extra batteries. Ghosts are believed to be electromagnetic in nature and can cause your batteries to run down rather quickly. Remember to bring batteries for both your flashlight and camera.

Cameras/Video Recorders: Cameras and video recorders are important tools for the modern ghost hunter today. A 35mm camera is an excellent camera to use because it can eliminate the chances of odd things showing up on the film, which can be caused by anomalies found on many digital cameras. Color film is the easiest to buy in stores, but black-and-white film and one-time use cameras are available as well. 400-, 800-, and 1000-speed film are the best choices. Black-and-white film and infrared films have been used for interesting results. Remember to bring extra rolls of film and batteries for the camera. Often, when you are on a ghost hunt, camera film and batteries malfunction (always happens to me) so make sure you are well stocked. You can use a camera tripod to help you eliminate moving the camera so that you can get a better picture. Make sure to advise your film developing company to develop your film as-is, as developers often think the pictures of ghosts are camera mistakes. When you are taking photographs, always remember to take off the camera strap so there is no chance it will get into the photo. Be sure to secure long hair too as this can get in the way.

Candles: If your flashlight and equipment stop working you may need to resort to candles and matches/lighters.

Cell Phone: Cell phones can be useful if you have an emergency and need to call for help, even though cell phones can also be affected by electromagnetic anomalies that can occur in the presence of a ghost, so be prepared.

Compass: Some people use a compass because the compass point may change in the presence of a spirit or ghost, and it too can be affected by an electromagnetic disturbance.

EMF (electromagnetic field) Detector: Likely the most important piece of equipment, an EMF detector will pick up electronic fields over various frequencies. A digital readout is preferred in an EMF detector, and some detectors have an alarm that will sound to alert you to sudden changes. The cost for this piece of equipment ranges from $40 to $150.

Tri-Field Natural EM Meter: Designed expressly for use in paranormal investigation, this amazingly sensitive device is one of the favorite portable instruments of researchers around the world. In the magnetic setting, the unit has a sensitivity of 2.5 milligausses, which is less than 0.5% of the earth's field. In the electric setting, it has a sensitivity of 3 volts-per-meter, which is well below the level at which static electricity (10,000 volts-per-meter) forms. This instrument has a setting that will alert the investigator to the earliest stages of paranormal manifestation. This meter can detect changes in electrical magnetic currents long before they become obvious to people. It will even detect approaching thunderstorms and the presence of a person behind a wall. The alarm tone is proportional to the amount of change in the field and can be set for any desired threshold and measures radio and microwave waves from 100 KHz to 3 GHz in milliwatts of energy.

Flashlights: Since a lot of ghost hunting is done at night in places like cemeteries and battlefields, it's imperative you have quality flashlights.

First Aid Kit: Take along a first aid kit just as a precaution in case someone gets injured on the ghost hunt. Old buildings, graveyards, and battlefields can be hazardous in the dark.

Film: Take lots of extra film with you on the ghost hunt. The electromagnetic discharges can affect your film and you may have to replace it. Use 200- to 1000-speed film, which will provide the best photographs in low light.

Gaussmeter or Cellsensor: An excellent tool for the modern ghost hunter, the *Cellsensor,* or gaussmeter, is a highly sensitive meter, which features both a cell phone frequency RF measurement, as well as a single axis ELF gaussmeter. The gaussmeter is calibrated around 50/60 Hz and also offers two scales: 0–5 and 0–50 mG. Remote probe with 2-foot extension cord allows the user greater flexibility and reach. Both RF and gaussmeter provide audio and a large flashing light that corresponds to field strength so you can hear and see in the dark when you are getting a positive reading. It includes complete documentation on how to conduct proper measurements.

Multidetector II: This measures electric and magnetic fields and is highly sensitive. It has power cables that can be extended more than one meter, and it is able to detect the presence of TVs, computers, and other electronic devices from a distance of more than three to four meters, and high voltage cables at more than 350 meters. It features an LED display, which provides a high luminosity to enable measurements even in dark areas like cellars, attics, and of course, graveyards.

Headset Communicators: Headset communicators can provide a method to communicate with your ghost-hunting party. This equipment is good for distant communication on a site and provides you with benefit of leaving your hands free to use your other equipment and to take notes.

Infrared Thermometer: A non-contact infrared thermometer emits an invisible infrared beam that reads the temperature of anything the beam comes in contact with. Researchers have found that this type of thermometer can detect cold spots, moving and stationary, in under a second.

Motion Detectors: A useful tool for ghost hunters. They work best when left in a room during the time that no investigator is present. Many motion detectors used by paranormal investigators project an infrared beam. When the beam is disrupted by spirits, an alarm will sound giving the investigator a clue that spirits may be present, and when switched to alarm mode, it will sound a siren when it detects motion up to thirty feet away. Includes optional wall-mount brackets.

Night-vision Scopes: Some people like to use night vision equipment on their ghost hunting expeditions. There are monocular and binocular types to choose from, but both are useful, especially in areas where there is absolutely no artificial light. Binocular types are a better choice because they add the benefit of depth perception. Night vision adapters are available to put on your cameras and camcorders, ranging in price.

Notebook and Pen: You need a notebook and pen to record your investigation, as it is vital to describe weather conditions, the temperature, and what happened on your ghost hunt. The ghost hunter will need to document EMF and Thermal Scanner readings. The date, time, and who was present on the ghost hunt, as well as what was seen, heard, or felt, are all important things to note for future investigations.

Omni-directional Microphones: An excellent tool when investigating for Electronic Voice Phenomena (EVP). Paranormal investigators recommend external microphones and the use of these microphones will make it possible to avoid tainting the recording with noises from the internal parts of the tape recorder. Omni-directional microphones are ideal because they pick up sounds from every direction equally and can be used with standard, micro cassette, and digital recorders.

Spotlights: Spotlights are always good because they can help you set up your equipment when it's dark, and they also give you an added level of security.

Tape or Digital Recorder: Take along a tape recorder to pick up

EVP. When you turn it on and let it run for the entire hunt or investigation, on occasion, strange, ghostly voices may be heard. Be sure to speak in a normal voice, as this will prevent confusion about whether your whisper was really a ghost. You may not always hear the voices during your investigation but if you review your tape afterward you may hear voices or other human-like sounds on the tape.

Thermometer-hygrometer: This indoor thermometer/hygrometer allows one temperature reading and checks the humidity. Complete with a digital humidity/temperature gauge, and able to read a humidity range of 20% to 90%, this device is an excellent addition. As high humidity can also have an effect on your camera and cause your photos to appear to have orbs or mist on them, this piece of equipment will prove useful.

Thermal Imaging Scope: This device provides you with an actual image of what your thermal scanner sees. It provides the exact shape of a particular temperature anomaly. If, for example, someone or something is walking behind a wall, you will see that person's shape and size.

Thermal Scanner: This device measures temperature changes instantly for a specific area. As temperature changes are common in haunted locations, the importance of this tool becomes clear. Infrared thermal scanners are equally beneficial, but they will cost more. Because ghosts are believed to be electromagnetic in nature and their materialization requires the use of energy, a noticeable change in temperature and atmosphere will take place. There may be a severe drop in temperature that could range from twenty degrees or more. "Cold spots" are good indications of what many believe to be a "portal" haunting, which can appear and disappear quickly, so this tool would also be a good choice.

Walkie-talkies: The new and improved walkie-talkie will provide the ghost hunter with a better method of communication during the ghost hunt. It also adds a better sense of security.

Watch: You need to take a watch with you on a ghost hunt to record the time when events take place.

Web Sites (ghost and haunting related): One of the best and most effective tools is the Internet. As important as the telephone today, the Internet and the massive database of ghost research and related web sites, both professional and novice, are all excellent sources of information, regional legends, folklore, as well as an outstanding source of photographs of alleged ghosts and spirits. Because there are literally thousands of paranormal-related web sites today and at least eighty in Florida alone, I have listed a few of the most notable organizations in Appendix C.

Appendix B

Glossary and Terminology

The following category represents some of the many terms used by ghost hunters, paranormal investigators, and parapsychologists today. Although these examples represent only a few of many such subjects, I have listed what I believe to be the most common terms used today.

Agent: A human being who is unaware that he or she is directing poltergeist activity. It is believed that a poltergeist or similar entity will attach itself to a child, often a female, as an agent.

Altered States of Consciousness: Any state of consciousness that is different, either altered or reduced, from a typical state of normal consciousness.

Amulet: An object believed to have the power to ward off evil spirits or other malevolent demons. It is usually in the shape of a charm or talisman worn around the neck.

Apparition: A disembodied soul or spirit from the deceased, which may be seen or heard as a supernatural appearance. Apparitions may appear and disappear very suddenly, seemingly at will. They may pass through walls, cast shadows, or produce a reflection in a mirror. They may appear real or sometimes foggy or completely transparent. Sometimes they are accompanied by smells or produce cold spots or drafts. Most apparitions seem to have some sort of purpose, such as communicating a message, and are therefore known as crisis apparitions. These entities usually appear during a severe family crisis such as when someone has died. A collective apparition refers to an apparition that is seen by more than one person.

Apport: When a solid object manifests in different locations, without physical assistance, supposedly by a spirit.

Astral Body: The soul of a person that is projected outside of his or her body, as if attached by an invisible umbilical cord.

Astral Plane: The level of existence through which spirits of the dead pass or a level of existence in which an astral projection travels naturally.

Astral Projection: The separation of the astral body or spirit body from the physical body. This astral body may travel in the astral plane and possibly beyond.

Aura: An energy field that surrounds all living creatures, supposedly captured by Kirlian photography.

Automatic Writing: This is communication via a spirit, wherein the spirit controls the writer's hand, usually performed by a medium or psychic who writes out the messages. This medium may not be conscious of what he or she is writing.

Automatism: Spontaneous muscular movement, believed to be caused by a ghost. Automatic writing is one example of this, as well as involuntary movements or spasms during sleep.

Banshee: A spirit or omen of death, usually indigenous to Scotland and Ireland. The banshee is more often heard than seen, and is almost always due to a death in a family.

Channeling: A form of communication wherein a spirit communicates and sometimes possesses a psychic medium. Popular in the 1980s. The entity being channeled is believed to be a deceased human being, angel, or demon.

Clairaudience: The psychic ability to hear sounds and voices normally not heard by most people.

Clairvoyance: The psychic ability to see objects, persons, places or events regardless of time or distance.

Conjuring: The process of calling preternatural forces into aid or action through the use of necromancy or black magic.

Discarnate: Existing outside a physical body, in spirit form, possibly in a form of astral projection.

Disembodied Spirit: A spirit functioning without the use of the physical body.

Doppelganger: Doppelgangers appear to be the ghostly duplicates of a living person. The doppelganger will often be invisible to that person, and in some cases that person will come upon his own doppelganger engaged in some future activity. Doppelgangers are traditionally believed to be omens of bad luck or death of the living counterpart.

Earthbound: Referring to a spirit trapped on the earthly plain against its will.

Ectoplasm: An unknown substance that emanates from the bodies of mediums, correlating to supernatural phenomena.

Elemental: A lesser spirit bound to the fundamentals of nature, such as earth, wind, water, and fire, or perhaps even seen as the remains of the dead.

Entity: A term used to describe a disembodied spirit or ghost of a preternatural reality.

Exorcism: The process of expelling or removing an evil spirit by a religious ceremony. Exorcisms may be performed by a priest, minister, rabbi, or shaman, each using similar ceremonies to disrupt or banish an evil spirit or entity.

Exorcist: One who conducts the rights of exorcism, such as a priest, rabbi, witch, or shaman.

ESP: Extra-Sensory Perception, or the ability to observe things that are beyond common levels of perception.

Ghost: A ghost can best be described as a form of spiritual recording, similar to an audio or videotape. Although there is no life force left, a ghost may replay the same scene or action over and over. A ghost may be the residual energy of a person, animal, or even an inanimate object, locked in repetition. It is widely believed that if a person has performed a repetitious act for a long period of time in life, he or she may leave a psychic impression or "psychic scent" in that area. This psychic scent may stay in the area long after the person who created it has moved on or died. This paranormal event is very vivid when first encountered and appears to be sentient. Over time, this psychic scent, or spirit will get weaker over time, but is believed it can recharge itself under the right circumstances.

There are many theories of what ghosts are. Many believe that ghosts are a residual energy left behind by a person of emotional strength or a person who wanted more life. Or they might be spirits that revolve around specific, traumatic life events. Many believe that there are various specific electromagnetic impulses that pulse and expend during periods of high excitement or stress, and that this energy may last long periods of time, or even feed on similar forms of electromagnetic energy, such as a power plant or other places where high levels of electricity pass. Some believe that ghosts are telepathic images. A particularly sensitive person, such as a psychic, may pick up or receive vibrations, most likely from strong past events and from the area where they occurred. Such an event may also explain instances where a person sees a loved one at the moment or near the moment of that loved one's death—the dying one might be unconsciously projecting their thoughts to a receptive person, such as a family member. It is also believed that ghosts could be the result of time slippage, where an event that happened in the past might be seen briefly in our present time because of a fluctuation in our space-time continuum.

Ghost Hunting or Investigating: When a person or group of people investigates a location where there have been alleged sightings of ghosts, attempting to find evidence of such existence. These people will use a wide variety of equipment to capture visual evidence, sounds, etc.

Ghost Lights: These anomalous balls of iridescent or glowing lights have also been called will o' the wisps, earthlights, and spook lights. They appear largely in the south and west United States, and are specific to one area or common location. Although sometimes dismissed as nothing more than swamp gas, ghost lights are reliable throughout the year and in some places these lights have been the subject of scientific study, such as the Greenbrier Lights in Jacksonville, Florida, and the Snow Hill Road Lights in Oviedo, Florida. Of the many theories and legends revolving around these mysterious lights, the typical folk tale involves ghostly, disgruntled Indian braves, phantom trains, and UFOs.

Ghostly Sounds and Lights: Sometimes a haunting will consist entirely of the sound of footsteps or ghostly music. There are also many legends of ghost lights, often said to be caused by a ghostly lantern, a spectral motorcycle, or a phantom train. The music heard at the Myrtle Hill Mausoleum in Ybor City, Florida, constitutes a phantom sound in the form of a muted but audible music box.

Ghost Ships: Although rare, these ghostly sea vessels have been seen throughout the ages, most notably the *Flying Dutchman*, or the ghostly burning ship of Block Island, Rhode Island, and the ghostly fishing ship of Mayport Village, Florida.

Haunted: In the context of parapsychology, a building, house, or area is considered "haunted" when paranormal activity can be documented repeatedly over a period of time. Paranormal activity, however, can vary dramatically from case to case and some paranormal activity is not associated with the presence of an entity or ghost.

Inhuman Spirit: An entity or spirit of a being that has never lived in the earthly realm, such as a demon.

Levitation: The raising of a body or object without any physical or visible means, found in some poltergeist cases and hauntings.

Magic/Magick: Not to be confused with stage magic, this is the art, science, and practice of producing supernatural effects in hopes of causing change to occur. The controlling of events in nature with one's own will.

Medium/Channeling Agent: A person claming to make contact with discarnate or inhuman spirits on the astral plane.

Occult: Pertaining to the supernatural, that which is beyond the range of natural knowledge.

Orbs: fast becoming the most common aspect of paranormal and ghost research, these faint balls of transparent light resemble magnified dust spores or droplets of water, and are known among parapsychological researchers as ghost orbs, spirit globules, and spirits in transit. Orbs are believed to be the main transportation mode for spirits because they require little energy in this state. One of the primary distinctions between ghosts and globules is that ghosts are imprints of the dead bound in an endless loop of repetition. Globules, in comparison, are mobile and very much sentient entities that can change their frequencies and locations at will.

Ouija Board: Oui meaning "yes" in French and *ja* meaning "yes" in German, the Ouija Board consists of letters of the alphabet, numbers one through ten, and the words "yes," "no," and "goodbye," and it is used as a tool for communicating with spirits. Although used by many as a game or form of entertainment, some feel that the Ouija Board is an unwise form of communication to take part in, as it may open up corridors or portals to unfriendly spirits or even demons.

Out of Body Experience: Also known as *Astral Projection,* it occurs when a person purposefully or unconsciously leaves his or her body in a spirit form.

Parapsychology: "Para" meaning "above or beyond" and "psychology" meaning the study of man, his psyche and the human condition. Parapsychology is the scientific study of phenomena that natural laws have not yet explained.

Pentagram: The magical diagram, such as the Seal of Solomon, consists of a five-pointed star, which is the representation of man, as well as the five elements. Considered by occultists to be the most potent means of conjuring spirits, the pentagram is said to protect against evil spirits.

Poltergeist: From the German meaning "noisy ghost." It is a spirit associated with the movement of objects and general mischievous activity. Poltergeists are the only spirits who may leave immediate physical traces and are best known for throwing things about and producing rapping sounds and other noises. Poltergeists often occur where there are children on the brink of puberty, and may often interact with people.

Preternatural: Associated with inhuman, demonic, or diabolical spirits or forces.

Psychic: Dealing with the ability to see, hear, feel, and sense beyond the average human ability. Includes mediums.

Psychic Cold Spot: The cold sensation received when a spirit is present, usually having defined boundaries.

Psychic Photograph: Supernatural or preternatural images appearing on a photograph, from ghostly images to orbs.

Psychical Research: The study of psychic phenomena, including earth-mysteries, ESP, and ghosts and hauntings.

Psychokinesis (PK): The movement of objects without the use of physical means, by using the mind.

Repetitious Spirits: Some apparitions are believed to repeat the same motions or scenes over and over with no apparent intelligence. Many classic hauntings fall into this category. Examples: The Lady in White seen walking the battlements of Derbyshire, England, or the Brown Lady of Raynham Hall, who is seen walking down a hallway with a swaying lantern; the ghostly seventeenth-century soldiers continuously fighting on the Marsden Moors in England and the ghostly sentry who walks guard on the Turnbull Fort in New Smyrna Beach, Florida.

Shadow People: A relatively newly discovered form of entity, said to be a nocturnal spirit, having human form, and prone to flickering on the walls and ceiling of houses and other structures. Frequently a subject of the *Art Bell Show,* the famous AM radio nighttime talk show, shadow people are believed to be evil in nature.

Specter: A ghost, or supernatural entity (see *Spirit*).

Spirit: A spirit is the actual living essence, or soul, of a person that has remained after the physical body has died. Spirits usually appear for one of three reasons. First, if a person died suddenly or with little warning, as in the case of a car accident, the victim may not actually realize that he or she is dead. Second, a person could be confined to this world by an unkept promise made to a loved one. Third, he or she may have some unfinished business, usually pertaining to a loved one. A variation of this reason would be if the person were murdered at an untimely point in his or her life. Spirits, unlike ghosts, can communicate with the living. Usually, if a person frequents a place where the deceased spent much of his or her time, a form of psychic communication can result. Sudden and unexplained feelings of sadness or melancholy are common indications, especially if encountered only in one particular room or area. Another way that a spirit can communicate with the living is through dreams. Although much more rare, a spirit can make itself appear as an apparition or make small items physically move.

Supernatural: An activity or event believed to be caused by a spirit or ghost, or even God or his angels. Used commonly to describe anything outside the bounds of natural laws.

Talisman/Charm: Also known as a fetch, these may be drawings of various shapes and sizes, which have specified purposes of good luck, protection, health, etc., and can be worn as a necklace or key chain (see *Amulet*).

Telekinesis: Telepathic sounds and voices projected to people.

Telepathy: Psychic communications between individuals.

Teleportation or apport: Objects moved or materialized by supernatural forces.

Will o' the Wisps: Also known as ghost lights, will o' the wisps are frequently assumed to be natural phenomena, such as pockets of swamp gas that hover and rise over swamps, ignite by natural causes, and glow blue or green. Also known as corpse candles, fox fire, elves' light and *ignis fatuus*, which is Latin for "foolish fire." Some believe these lights to be omens of bad luck or death.

Vortex Phenomenon: A traveling form of ghostly energy.

Appendix C
Ghost Research Organizations

The following is a listing of the most prominent psychical research organizations devoted to scientific inquiry, parapsychology, and paranormal research today. Several of these organizations, such as the American Society for Psychical Research, are membership-based institutes, but may share resources with non-members. Several of these societies also publish online journals and printed periodicals in the field of parapsychology and paranormal research, which may be of interest to Florida ghost hunters. The Florida-based web sites herein are an excellent resource for organized ghost hunts, investigative studies, and ghost-hunting tours throughout the state of Florida.

American Society for Psychical Research (ASPR): www.aspr.com

Society for Psychical Research (SPR): www.spr.ac.uk

The International Consortium for Psychical Research and Paranormal Investigation (ICPRPI), Department of Folklore and Urban Legends E-mail: Arkham1964@gmail.com

Psychical Research Foundation
c/o William G. Roll, Psychology Department, West Georgia College: www.psychicalresearchfoundation.com/papers.html

Psychic Research Foundation: www.psychic-research.org.uk/

Parapsychological Association, Inc.: www.parapsych.org

Parapsychology Foundation: www.parapsychology.org

The Parapsychology Research Group:
http://hopelive.hope.ac.uk/psychology/para/links.html

Foundation for Research on the Nature of Man, Institute for Parapsychology
The Institute of Noetic Sciences: www.noetic.org/

Graduate Parapsychology Program: Department of Holistic Studies Division of

Perceptual Studies, University of Virginia:
www.healthsystem.virginia.edu/internet/personalitystudies/home.cfm

Center for Scientific Anomalies Research (CSAR):

P.O. Box 1052 Ann Arbor, MI 48103

www.answers.com/topic/center-for-scientific-anomalies-research

Society for Scientific Exploration: www.scientificexploration.org

Committee for Skeptical Inquiry, or CSI
   (formerly the Committee for the Scientific Investigation of Claims of the
   Paranormal, or CSICOP): www.csicop.org

Association for the Scientific Study of Anomalous Phenomenal: www.assap.org

Coast-to-Coast Radio: www.coasttocoastam.com A great late-night AM
   radio show hosted by George Noory that offers tales of the unknown,
   stories of strange monsters, and of course, lots of ghost stories that will
   keep the listener thinking throughout the night.

The Center for Paranormal Research and Investigation:
   http://virginiaghosts.com

Daytona Beach Paranormal Research Group: www.dbprginc.org

Florida Ghost Chapter: www.floridaghostchapter.com

Florida Paranormal Research Foundation: www.floridaparanormal.com

Haunts of the World's Most Famous Beach (Daytona Beach, FL):
   http://www.hauntsofdaytona.com/

Haunted Places Directory: www.haunted-places.com/

International Ghost Hunters Society: www.ghostweb.com/

Nightwolf Paranormal Research:
   http://members.tripod.com/LABTEC7/home.htm

Obiwan's UFO-Free Paranormal Page: www.ghosts.org An excellent site
   with hundreds of resources for ghost hunters everywhere.

The Paranormal Yellow Pages: http://parapages.ning.com An excellent resource
   for many Florida ghost hunters, as well as organizations nationwide.

The Shadowlands: www.theshadowlands.net A very well done page on many
   aspects of the paranormal, including an extensive section on ghosts and
   hauntings.

Appendix D
Ghost Tours

Ghost tours, or ghost walks, have become all but customary in many cities throughout the United States today. Most of these groups are designed around the haunted or ghostly history of a particular location, usually a location of some historical significance. Sometimes, these walking tours are specifically designed to be entertaining accounts of speculative incidents that may revolve around a ghost or haunting. On occasion, these tours will cover actual, documented histories that report paranormal activity, but most often, they will embellish an actual story or legend, thus furthering an urban legend.

This process of telling a good story, and making a little money as a result of that story, may alone prove to be the hobgoblin to the serious paranormal and psychical researcher, as well as the scholarly folklorist. So, with this said, I would like to recommend caution when braving the busy streets and downtowns in search of ghosts. Although your guide might be wearing a top hat and a flowing black cape, and his or her story may sound wonderfully exciting, please keep in mind that there may be more falsehoods in his anecdote than facts. Although entertaining, there is always the possibility that the story is incorrect or simply designed to capture your attention, and your money. Therefore, respectfully, unless your guide holds at least a master's degree in either folklore, history, or parapsychology, take the story with a grain of salt and do the research for yourself. You might be surprised what you'll find.

The following is a list of southern and central Florida's ghost walks and haunted tours. Bear in mind, however, that some groups may have closed their businesses and new ones may not be publicly advertising yet. The best way to learn of new ghost tours in your area is by the World Wide Web or by calling your city's chamber of commerce.

Amelia Island

"Old Towne Carriage Company" offers a professionally guided, narrated walking tour through historical Fernandina Beach. With tales of the supernatural, each show will introduce you to north Florida's spookier past. The guides are local residents who have a love of both history and the supernatural, combining the two interests to give you a thrilling tour filled with historical and haunted facts.

For more information, call: 904-277-1555. Or visit their website at: www.ameliacarriagetours.com

St. Augustine

Ancient City Tours

Ancient City Tours, Inc., offers tours of the city's oldest house, haunted buildings, and many historical cemeteries on the "Ghostly Gathering" carriage tour.

They also host "A Ghostly Encounter" walking tour, which begins at the Spanish Military Hospital Museum, where guests will learn of the advanced medical practices of the Spanish colonists, and takes you throughout the haunted streets of St. Augustine. For more information on times and prices for each tour, call: 904-827-0807 or 800-597-7177.

Ghost Tours of St. Augustine

For more information on times and prices for any of the following three tours, call: 1-888-461-1009 or 904-829-1122. Or visit the Ghost Tours of St Augustine website at: www.ghosttoursofstaugustine.com.

"Walking Tour"

The "A Ghostly Experience" walking tour leads participants through the historic back streets and ancient cobblestone alleys of St. Augustine by lantern light. Guides in period costumes will periodically stop to share tales from the tombstones. All of the stories are researched through records from historical libraries, church documents, personal diaries and personal interviews. Tales begin at dusk and last a little more than an hour. Moreover, this award-winning tour is held every night of the year, including all holidays, with other seasonal and private tours available.

"Riding Tour"

Board the "Ghosts & Legends" riding tour for an unforgettable passage into the night. On this journey, guests travel along old city streets to antiquated sites and to the haunted lighthouse to experience some of St. Augustine's most frightening locations. Guides share accounts of unsolved mysteries and murders, scandalous tales, and ghostly sightings, along with intimate details of our nation's oldest city.

"Sailing Tour"

The "Ghosts of Matanzas" sailing tour is for the sea and ghost lover in all of us, as guests set sail aboard the magnificent 72-foot schooner *Freedom* for a one-hour cruise on the bay. The leisurely tour offers guests the chance to look up through the blowing sails and gaze at the stars as the ship glides through the dark haunted waters and while a ghostly host spins tall tales, sings songs and interacts with the "crew."

Ghost Augustine's Ghost Store & Tours

GhoSt Augustine Ltd Co., operated by Jonas Brihammar, has put a unique twist on the ghost hunting and touring business by offering the city's own "Haunted Pub Tours" and "Haunted Hearse Ride." His company also offers use of the renowned K-II EMF Meter (ghost and anomaly detecting device) for every tour.

The "Haunted Pub Tours" gives guests a chance to ride in one of their two old gothic hearses with a licensed tour guide and fellow pub crawlers to visit haunted locations throughout the ancient city, as well as the St. Augustine Lighthouse. Guests visit three or more pubs on their journey, spending approximately 30 minutes inside each pub so as to allow time to digest the chilling story about the establishment, and perhaps even a drink (drinks are not included in the ticket price).

For more information on times and prices for each tour, call: 866-266-6641. Or check out their web site at: www.ghostaugustine.com.

Haunted St. Augustine

Dr. Harry C. Stafford, Ph.D., who produces a no-nonsense and highly educational experience into the unknown, leads this tour. Guests have the chance to take part in active investigations and learn to use actual ghost-hunting equipment that may in fact detect the presence of ghosts, apparitions, and poltergeist activity.

For more information on session times and prices call: 904-823-9500 or 904-687-4232. Or visit: www.haunted-st-augustine.com.

Pensacola

The Historic Pensacola Village

The Historic Pensacola Village offers tours around their quaint township which highlight some of the creepy folklore and legends surrounding this Victorian village. Patrons have the chance to explore some of the beautiful historic homes here and to hear the interesting history of each in the process. Guests also have the opportunity to visit other popular sites throughout the region, including the T.T. Wentworth, Jr. Museum and Old Christ Church. Tours last anywhere from one to three hours.

Pensacola Historical Society

For almost twenty years, the Pensacola Historical Society has been conducting "Haunted House Walking and Trolley Tours" on the two weekends before Halloween in October. These tours are a favorite of young and old, native and tourist alike. Tickets go on sale the third week in September, so be sure to call early, as tickets sell fast.

Interested in reading more about Pensacola's haunted history? Read *Ghosts, Legends and Folklore of Old Pensacola*. Look for a copy in the Pensacola Historical Museum Store. For more information on all tours and Pensacola destinations, call: 805-595-5985. Or write for an information guide to: West Florida Historic Preservation, Inc., P.O. Box 12866, Pensacola, FL 32591.

Bibliography

Clearfield, Dylan. *Floridaland Ghosts*. Michigan: Prism Stempien Thomas, 2000.

Guiley, Rosemary Ellen. *The Encyclopedia of Ghosts and Spirits*. New York: Facts on File, 1992.

Harvey, Karen. *Oldest Ghosts: St. Augustine Haunts*. Sarasota: Pineapple Press, 2000.

Hiller, Herbert L. *Guide to the Small and Historic Lodgings of Florida*. Pineapple Press, 1986.

Kermeen, Frances. *Ghostly Encounters: True Stories of America's Haunted Inns and Hotels*. Warner Books, 2002.

Lapham, Dave. *Ancient City Hauntings*. Sarasota: Pineapple Press, 2004.

Lapham, Dave. *Ghosts of St. Augustine*. Sarasota: Pineapple Press, 1997.

Powell, Jack. *Haunting Sunshine*. Sarasota: Pineapple Press, 2001.

Slone, David L. *Ghosts of Key West*. Key West: Phantom Press, 1998.

Spencer, John and Tony Wells. *Ghost Watching: The Ghosthunters' Handbook*. Great Britain: Virgin Books, 1995.

Miller, Capt. Bill. *Tampa Triangle: Dead Zone*. Saint Petersburg: Ticket to Adventure, Inc. 1997.

Montz, Larry and Deana Smoller. *ISPR Investigates the Ghosts of New Orleans*. Pennsylvania: Whitford Press, 2000.

Moore, Joyce Elson. *Haunt Hunter's Guide to Florida*. Sarasota: Pineapple Press, 1998.

Myers, Arthur. *The Ghostly Register*. Chicago: Contemporary Books, 1986.

Myers, Arthur. *Ghosts of the Rich and Famous*. Chicago: Contemporary Books, 1988.

Sources:

The May Stringer House, Brooksville

Anonymous, interviews by author, 2001, 2002.

Powell, Jack. *Haunting Sunshine.* Sarasota: Pineapple Press, 2001.

Silver Springs, Ocala

Anonymous, Strange Florida, *www.strangeflorida.com,* 2000.

Anonymous, interview by author, 2001.

Herlong Mansion, Micanopy

www.herlong.com

Hauck, Dennis William. *Haunted Places: The National Directory, A Guidebook to Ghostly Abodes, Sacred Sites, UFO Landings, and Other Supernatural Locations.* New York: The Penguin Group, 1996.

Powell, Jack. *Haunting Sunshine.* Sarasota: Pineapple Press, 2001.

Hotel Blanche, Lake City

Anonymous, interview by author, 2003.

School Four, Jacksonville

Anonymous, interviews by author, 2001, 2002.

Carriage House Apartments, Jacksonville

Anonymous, interviews by author, 2000, 2002.

Homestead Restaurant, Jacksonville

Hauck, Dennis William. *Haunted Places: The National Directory, A Guidebook to Ghostly Abodes, Sacred Sites, UFO Landings, and Other Supernatural Locations.* New York: The Penguin Group, 1996.

Powell, Jack. *Haunting Sunshine.* Sarasota: Pineapple Press, 2001.

Casa Marina Hotel, Jacksonville

Anonymous, interview by author, 2002, 2003.

Mayport Village, Mayport

Anonymous, interview by author, 2001.

Sunland Hospital North, Tallahassee

Anonymous, interviews by author, 2000, 2001.

Castillo de San Marcos, St. Augustine

Anonymous, interview by author, 2001.

Hauck, Dennis William. *Haunted Places: The National Directory, A Guidebook to Ghostly Abodes, Sacred Sites, UFO Landings, and Other Supernatural Locations.* New York: The Penguin Group, 1996.

Powell, Jack. *Haunting Sunshine.* Sarasota: Pineapple Press, 2001.

The Old Spanish Hospital, St. Augustine

Anonymous, interviews by author, 2002, 2003.

Flagler College, Ponce Hall, St. Augustine

Anonymous, interviews by author, 2002, 2003.

Clearfield, Dylan. *Floridaland Ghosts.* Michigan: Prism Stempien Thomas, 2000.

Casa Monica Hotel, St. Augustine

Anonymous, interview by author, 2003.

www.casamonica.com, 2004.

St. Francis Inn, St. Augustine

Anonymous, interview by author, 2003.

Harvey, Karen. *Oldest Ghosts: St. Augustine Haunts.* Sarasota: Pineapple Press, 2000.

Casa de la Paz St. Augustine

Anonymous, interview by author, 2003.

Casablanca Inn, St. Augustine

Anonymous, interview by author, 2003.

Clearfield, Dylan. *Floridaland Ghosts.* Michigan: Prism Stempien Thomas, 2000.

Harvey, Karen. *Oldest Ghosts: St. Augustine Haunts.* Sarasota: Pineapple Press, 2000.

Powell, Jack. *Haunting Sunshine.* Sarasota: Pineapple Press, 2001.

Harry's Seafood Bar and Grille, St. Augustine

Anonymous, interview by author, 2003.

Harvey, Karen. *Oldest Ghosts: St. Augustine Haunts.* Sarasota: Pineapple Press, 2000.

Clearfield, Dylan. *Floridaland Ghosts.* Michigan: Prism Stempien Thomas, 2000.

The Florida School for the Deaf and the Blind, St. Augustine

Anonymous, interviews by author, 2002, 2003.

Huguenot Cemetery, St. Augustine

Anonymous, interviews by author, 2002, 2003.

Harvey, Karen. *Oldest Ghosts: St. Augustine Haunts.* Sarasota: Pineapple Press, 2000.

Lapham, Dave. *Ghosts of St. Augustine.* Sarasota: Pineapple Press, 1997.

The Old Jail, St. Augustine

Anonymous, interview by author, 2003.

St. Augustine Lighthouse, St. Augustine

Anonymous, interview by author, 2003.

Moore, Joyce Elson. *Haunt Hunter's Guide to Florida.* Sarasota: Pineapple Press, 1998.

www.staugustinelighthouse.com

Taylor, Thomas. *Florida Lighthouse Trail.* Sarasota: Pineapple Press, 2001.

Index

Here are some other books from Pineapple Press on related topics. For a complete catalog, visit our website at www.pineapplepress.com. Or write to Pineapple Press, P.O. Box 3889, Sarasota, Florida 34230-3889, or call (800) 746-3275.

Florida's Ghostly Legends and Haunted Folklore, Volume 1: South and Central Florida; and *Florida's Ghostly Legends and Haunted Folklore, Volume 3: The Gulf Coast and Pensacola* by Greg Jenkins. The history and legends behind a number of Florida's haunted locations, plus bone-chilling accounts taken from firsthand witnesses of spooky phenomena. Volume 1 locations include the fortress ruins in New Smyrna Beach, Tampa's Myrtle Hill Cemetery, and the Biltmore Hotel. Volume 3 covers the historic city of Pensacola and continues southward through the Tampa area, Sarasota, and Naples. (pb)

Florida Ghost Stories by Robert R. Jones. Stories of ghosts and spirits and tall tales of strange happenings fill this volume. If they don't give you goose bumps and make your hair stand on end, at least they will offer you food for thought. (pb)

The Ghost Orchid Ghost and Other Tales from the Swamp by Doug Alderson. Florida's famous swamps serve as fitting backdrops for these chilling original stories. Who but a naturalist can really scare you about what lurks in the swamp? From the Author's Notes at the end of each story, you can learn a thing or two about Florida's swamps, creatures, and history, along with storytelling tips. (pb)

Haunt Hunter's Guide to Florida by Joyce Elson Moore. Discover the general history and "haunt" history of numerous sites around the state where ghosts reside. (pb)

Haunting Sunshine by Jack Powell. Take a wild ride through the shadows of the Sunshine State in this collection of deliciously creepy stories of ghosts in the theaters, churches, and historic places of Florida. (pb)

Haunted Lighthouses and How to Find Them, Second Edition by George Steitz. The producer of the popular TV series *Haunted Lighthouses* takes you on a tour of America's most enchanting and mysterious lighthouses. This updated edition has four new haunted lighthouses. (pb)

Ancient City Hauntings by Dave Lapham. In this sequel to *Ghosts of St. Augustine,* the author takes you on more quests for supernatural experiences through the dark, enduring streets of the Ancient City. Come visit the Oldest House, the Old Jail, Ripley's, the Oldest School House, all the many haunted B&Bs, and more. (pb)

Ghosts of St. Augustine by Dave Lapham. The unique and often turbulent history of America's oldest city is told in twenty-four spooky stories that cover four hundred years' worth of ghosts. (pb)

Oldest Ghosts by Karen Harvey. In St. Augustine (the oldest settlement in the New World), the ghost apparition are as intriguing as the city's history. (pb)